Atravesando

Aster(ix) Journal

presents

Atravesando

***

Edited by
Angie Cruz and Oindrila Mukherjee

BLUE SKETCH PRESS | PITTSBURGH

See page 174 for individual copyright information.

www.bluesketchpress.com
www.facebook.com/bluesketchpress.com

www.asterixjournal.com
www.facebook.com/asterixjournal

Atravesando: An Aster(ix) Anthology / Aster(ix) Journal
Edited by Angie Cruz and Oindrila Mukherjee — 1st ed.
ISBN (print) 978-1-942547-01-3 (trade paperback)

Cover Art by Adriana E. Ramírez based on a photo by Bunker Glosiempre, "Atravesando espejos."
More information on both available at www.aeramirez.com and www.flickr.com/photos/46974301@N00/ respectively.
Design by Little Owl Creative, www.littleowlcreative.com
Edited by Joseph N. Welch, III.

First Edition: March 2016

Printed in the United States of America
9 8 7 6 5 4 3 2 1

Contents

Editors' Note

Angie Cruz and Oindrila Mukherjee

This anthology of fiction and poetry embraces the themes of breaking through and crossing over. Our writers hail from all over the country—many of whom inhabit liminal spaces, embodying and evoking Gloria Anzaldua's borderlands, where the "borders" are often indistinguishable and the characters live in multiple worlds simultaneously. The stories and poems challenge and reveal to us what we trade when we love or are made to love, when we move or are forced to move, and how it feels when we experience an unexpected loss. Characters dream of lottery tickets, driving a car, being truly loved; rubber plants, suitcases and misbehaving men who are ripped apart; roosters, husbands and children die. The daughters of Bible-thumping and manipulative mothers, as well as stubborn and ambitious fathers, struggle and succeed to carve a space of their own.

This book is a true cornucopia of humor, tragedy and sensuality. Each and every work in this issue has unhinged us as editors in some way. We invite you to travel the world with these fierce female protagonists.

Enjoy!

Love Story for a Foreign Girl

Fiona Cheong

1.

Tell yourself, at least he's kind. You don't know this for sure, but the odds are good—look at all his gifts. Roses yesterday (not cheap), Hershey's Kisses today (too obvious). You'll realize this one day far in the future, but for now, you're nineteen and only six months out of your father's house—what do you care? Tell yourself that Americans don't beat their wives—you know this because you've seen it on TV—in America, husbands buy their wives diamond rings, cruise ship tickets, Maytag washing machines, and say "I love you" on the phone. In America, husbands and wives kiss in public, call each other "Baby," go away on second honeymoons. Actually, you have witnessed none of it yourself, but any day now, you believe you will.

This one, he's not quite what you were expecting, but he's all right, weight and height notwithstanding. Tell yourself he's not fat, he's stocky—just a little on the heavy side. He's also not tall, not even by Singaporean standards—the first time he came up to you in the cafeteria line, you were looking him straight in the eye, which means he's not even as tall as your tallest cousin, who with your other cousins have remained on the other side of the Pacific—but then, what do you need a tall one for? Looks aren't supposed to matter and you're not superficial. Remind yourself you're not superficial, having been raised among temples and oranges offered on red kitchen altars to the Buddha of Great Compassion. Remind yourself, at Thaipusam, your neighbors walked unscathed on hot coals during the festivities, their skeletal shoulders bare beneath the equatorial sun. That's the world you're from, not this America of plump skin and overwhelming dinner portions and expensive bits of clothing protecting almost nothing. Remind yourself whose daughter you are, whose granddaughter, whose niece, whose pupil.

"You have such a spiritual face," he tells you, his middle finger on a slow expedition up the inside of your thigh. No other guy has ever tried to get this far with you and when he flicks back the hem of your panties and slips in at the crotch, you're wetter than you thought you'd be. His finger wiggles around the mouth of your vagina, warm and thick as a cocktail sausage. You're not sure if you want to go on—you think, maybe not, because suddenly he's leaning close and his breath on your face makes you claustrophobic. Say nothing. Think about the time your cousins lowered you in the wooden bucket, farther and farther down the old church well. "Sekali jatoh, then how?" your aunts scolded the eldest, Gabriel, who was thirteen at the time, when they found out. You had thought it, too, in the well—you had thought that you might fall, the cold air plastered to your neck like mold. You survived that. You can survive this.

(No one's told you, yet, that sex doesn't have to be survived so meanwhile) tell yourself he's kind, not stingy with his money where you're concerned. Besides, he's gentle with his fingers, and since no guy's ever gotten this far with you, feel free to mistake surprises for pleasure. Let him slide one finger in, then two. Forgive the accidental scrape of nail, the searing heat of sudden blood. Someday, everything about him will become ordinary. This figment of knowledge presses on your chest, clogs your throat like dust—voices from another room thicken in your ears, threading you back to your father's house. So look up, while you can, at Orion's Belt spreading so gloriously behind the maple leaves. At the first clink of buckle, bite your lower lip. Breathe slowly when he unzips. Turn your cheek to the ground and smell this American grass against your hair.

There are women everywhere who are alone—spinsters like your Koko Mathilda even though she's gorgeous, widows like some of your other aunts who will never re-marry.

Tell yourself you're lucky.

Later, when washing your panties in the dormitory sink, gaze in the mirror. Find his words in your mother's expression that everyone who's known you since you were a child says you carry in your eyes. *You have such a spiritual face.* Against the bated fluorescent breath of this fall night on a university campus at the edge of your new world, follow the rise of your family's cheekbones, the compressed triangle of your father's nose, the mild downturn of his lips. No one has ever called you *pretty*, though an uncle did comment, once, on your pleasant smile. *Pretty* was reserved for your cousins Maureen, Noreen and Doreen, Gabriel's sisters who helped lower you down the well. You are no fool. You're aware that *pleasant* isn't the same as *pretty*, and neither is *spiritual.* But *spiritual* has brought you flowers and chocolates and who knows what else is waiting up ahead? Spiritual brought you an actual date, with a movie and popcorn thrown in, and someone wanting to make love to you under the stars. So *spiritual* is all right. More than all right.

Pay attention now. You don't know it, yet, but here's your formative moment. You're not superficial. You're spiritual, because as you will soon learn, your past is *the East*, full of the rustle of beaded screens swinging between what's real and not real. Your past is Susie Wong, Marco Polo, a twilight without geography. Pay attention. This is the mystery that you are on the brink of becoming in America. It's your ticket into the American heart.

2.

Now the going gets tricky. You've got to get serious about your accent, that ocean lilt from the other room, English pronounced as if it weren't English, your family's British Commonwealth grammar all mixed up. Your Koko Stella complaining about your youngest uncle and his girlfriend, about their exhibitionist behavior, how they're always hugging and fawning over each other. "T'ak seronoh, those two. Every time they go jalan, must pulok-pulok. Sudah kena spotted-lah, last night. And by whom, you know? By Madam Big Mouth herself. You see-lah, boleh mati, t'ak?" Koko Stella, your father's married sister, your mother's kindergarten friend and Gabriel's mother, bustles around inside your head, her voice pumping you full of memory. She wears batik colors and a hair net, smokes cigars with your uncles and has almost nothing good to say about the younger generation, except when it comes to you. You she loved, too obviously and too much. Don't forget that old church well, the receding circle of afternoon sky, your cousins' faces peering down in shadow. Tell yourself it's okay to let go. Start with Koko Stella. When putting her in a story for Creative Writing 202, catch every "lah" in mid-flow. Leaping as it did from another language, anyway, the word is merely pace—untranslatable. Slice it off. Koko Stella would want you to let go. Wouldn't she? She would want you to build a life, make the most of your time in America, be happy. You suspect she'd feel differently if she knew you wouldn't be going back, so don't tell anyone you won't be going back. Don't tell anyone you've already got yourself a boyfriend, who's stocky, not fat, and says "I love you" on the phone, and calls you "Baby" in bed. They won't guess if you don't tell. You're twenty and barely two years out of your father's house. You haven't even lost your accent, though you've learned to dangle "cool" and "dude" and "whassup" off your sentences like Navajo silver, as if you were some

Asian chick from California.

You've learned to high five.

While no one's looking, read *The Woman Warrior*, *House on Mango Street*, and *Notes of a Native Son*. Read *The Way to Rainy Mountain*. In coffee houses, on the bus, in the aisles at K-Mart, count to yourself the number of Americans with bones like the bones of faces that help you sleep. Eventually, when you close your eyes, you will not miss the lullaby of frogs in the long grass, the billowing fragrance of orchids and frangipani and the gamelan call of the bamboo. You will forget that incense no longer wafts up the stairs, floating prayers for prosperity and health past your door.

Tell yourself it's all for the best. Remind yourself, you want the future more than memory.

Get used to the phrase, "people of color." Think of yourself as "we." When asked, "Where are you from?" if your boyfriend's not around, say, "San Francisco." Say, "Seattle." Say, "Queens, New York." Any one of these will do. When asked, "But where are your parents from?" say, "San Francisco." Say, "Seattle." Say, "Queens, New York."

Always answer the phone when it rings. When your boyfriend asks, "Don't you think it's time you told them?" tell him you will, soon. When he says, "Don't you want to get married?" don't panic. Remember that Europeans have been imagining the East for generations—you have an entire culture to use as an excuse. Say, "My father's very Chinese. He needs some time to get used to the idea of my marrying a non-Chinese." Don't tell him about your father's blondie girlfriend—how on your fourteenth birthday, your father came home drunk with a new German secretary from the office who giggled and blurted out her name, *Regina*, (a hard *g*), while your aunts were handing out slices of cake to your classmates and Sister Marie, who taught music and folk dancing during the week, and aikido on Saturdays, was putting Barry Manilow on the turntable. Your boyfriend will ask, "How much time?"

and perhaps you'll feel a window springing open, an opportunity for escape. Don't take it. You don't know enough about the quality of the other fish in the sea, the ones available to you—keep in mind, no one has yet called you pretty.

Say, "Do you love me? Do you love me enough to wait?" It'll buy you a bit of time. Meanwhile, write *hard, card, marred, Harvard, tarpaulin,* on a blank page in your checkbook and carry this with you everywhere. Practice enunciating these words at least six times a day. Roll the *r* on the fleshy middle of your tongue, not too harshly—just a soft purr like the crawl of waves on a windless afternoon.

It's a delicate balance: You're spirit ual, but you don't want to be F.O.B. You may be *Third World,* or *Oriental,* or just plain exotic, but you sure as hell don't want to be *Fresh Off the Boat.*

3.

So it happens sooner than you expect. That's all right. You've had your own fantasies for a while—you can't get wet without them anymore, which Louella Ruiz, who's from Austin, Texas, and is your best friend here, tells you is absolutely normal. What Louella means is: Of course, everything about a lover will become ordinary. "It's never like it was at the beginning, Anna," she says, her black hair blacker than yours in the wintry light, her voice like a bell in the chilled December air. Louella's not much older than you, but has been married since she was sixteen and lives in the apartment next-door with Miguel, who makes good money as a chef in the fancy French restaurant near the campus. Louella and Miguel were high school sweethearts and have a daughter, Sasha, who's five and wants to be an Olympic gymnast when she grows up. They call you "Anna"—it's the name you go by—only your boyfriend still calls you "Su Chin" (you realized too late, you never should have shown him your passport), and only in the letters from home, people still say, "Dear Gemok," or, if it's one of your cousins writing, especially Doreen (who's just gotten engaged and in a year will marry into one of the wealthiest families on the island), she'll use the English version, "Dear Fatso," which irritates you because it's not as if you haven't long shed your pubescent fat. By American standards, you're even skinny. Still, it's not Doreen's fault she doesn't know this. You haven't been home in three years and you've ignored the various ways people have found to ask, "Why?" You can't even send home photographs taken with your boyfriend's camera—the ones of you alone, clothed. Your father wouldn't notice a thing, but your aunts, especially Koko Stella, and Koko Mathilda, who seldom spoke but gazed out of windows with such attentiveness throughout your childhood—they've watched you since the hour you were born. Koko Stella held you while your mother bled beneath the dazzling hospital lights. (Your father, you've heard, wasn't even there.) Show your aunts a photograph of you now, and they might begin to guess. So it's all right. Forgive yourself, and them, for what you must do. Send home only your semester grades. Send home brief, poker-faced aerograms. Add a picture postcard now and then for variety. And always sign yourself, "Gemok." When you feel the urge to spill the truth, you've got Louella. She doesn't smell like any of your aunts, but her arms are warm and sincere, and conversations with her carry no complications.

"What you've got to decide is," says Louella, "are you still in love with him? If you are, then both of you have got to work this out, whatever it takes. Know what I mean?"

You know what she means. Conversations like the one you and Louella are having have taken place before, are taking place, all over the world, and nowadays even on TV. (You've seen the interviews. You understand, there will always be women who have it worse than you.) When you found the earring in your boyfriend's pocket last week, there was nothing unique about that—a single earring, good-luck jade, a sheen of green not commonly available in American Chinatowns. You never wear jade. (Too F.O.B.) Nothing unique about your racing heart when you put it back, dropping the earring slowly in his pocket like something fragile, possibly precious, irreplaceable. When you counted the condom packets in his dresser drawer, there was nothing unique about the fact that too many were missing. And in the mirror, your face was a face you've seen before, long ago in your father's house.

What puzzles you is the hurt. Why should any of it still hurt? It's not as if your own mind hasn't wandered during sex over the last few months.

"Of course it hurts," says Louella. "Some bitch has got her fingers in your pie, Girlfriend. That always matters. So my question to you is, do you still love your man?"

The question is huge.

These last few months, you've lingered in the bathroom longer after sex, taking longer to wash off. There's a Cuban with eyelashes to die for who saunters past you every Tuesday afternoon in Shakespeare 330, on his way to the back row. All faded dungarees and muscle, biceps blossoming in white T-shirt cut-off sleeves, a smile so sweet, you're blushing every time you catch his eye. You've told Louella his name. Joaquin. You're friends with his best friend Mikey. They're all from Newark, New Jersey—Mikey, Joaquin, and the girlfriend Celia (who works at K-Mart and doesn't attend the university)—it's where they grew up after their families came over. You've seen Celia. She's gorgeous like Koko Mathilda, the kind of gorgeous that hushes a room and renders almost every kind of man speechless. It's beyond losing weight, beyond using the right make-up and having a good haircut and wearing the right colors. It can be dangerous, that kind of gorgeous, and now you think maybe for Koko Mathilda it was—something happened to her before you were born, the shape of which hovers like a ghost no one will mention in your father's house. You've told Louella you don't mind that you can never be that gorgeous. You know in real life, a fish like Joaquin will always swim way beyond your reach. You've told her he helps you out, anyway (wink, wink)—in the bathroom after sex.

Only lately, even that hasn't worked.

Say, "I don't know," this time, even if it makes your voice faint, so faint, Louella's leaning toward you over the ginger cookies and the banana bread, her dark eyes frowning. She's good at feeling people out, so she knows something's up. What she doesn't know is that you don't know exactly what's up. You would tell her if you could, because you want to tell somebody. You want somebody to know that the ground's no longer firm beneath your feet—it's been gathering water, sea grasses, whirlpools.

And it's been happening for a while, before last week, which is why last week shouldn't matter. And yet, it does. So say again, "I don't know," because that's as close to the truth as you can bear to be for now.

Breathe in. Count one, two, three. Breathe out. Smile and withdraw. Pretend you're on *Donohue* or *Oprah*. Add: "He's been good to me, except for this. You know how he is. He's a kind person. We're just under a lot of stress. You know we're applying to grad schools. I mean, his top choice is Harvard Law, and there are good writing programs in Boston but what if I could get into Iowa? Or Stanford? Or Cornell? Having to choose is just so stressful."

"So what does that mean? You're going to try and work it out?" asks Louella, her tone lumpy as fudge because she'd rather just cut to the chase.

You don't want to lose her friendship by lying, so don't. Shrug your shoulders but not blithely. Say again, "I don't know." Cut yourself a chunk of banana bread, wielding the knife carefully because it's after five o'clock. The sun's gone down, but neither of you has moved to turn on the light. Breathe slowly, evenly, the way Sister Marie once taught you. Breathe as if your heart's still whole.

4.

Wait until daylight, after you've had some sleep, and your boyfriend's out of the apartment again. You'll want your wits about you so the break is clean. You'll want to pack only what you need, but also everything you'll need, so you won't have to come back and risk dragging matters out. If you came back, you might change your mind, end up staying, end up trying to work things out.

It's not as if anyone has yet called you *pretty*, but lately, fewer and fewer Americans have been asking you where you're from. You're almost four years out of your father's house. You've learned how to fade your dungarees just right, and to call them "blue jeans" in public. You wear Timberlands in the snow and a Yankees baseball cap in summer. You no longer hunch your shoulders when you're in a bikini. You shave your legs. You sunbathe.

Most important of all: a famous and respected writer who on Friday visited the fiction workshop you're in told you later, at a reception being held in his honor, that he found your story (a half-true, half-made-up story about Koko Mathilda) fascinating. He called it "deeply engaging." He called you "highly gifted." He gave you his phone number in New York City and said, "If you happen to be in the city, call. We'll have dinner."

Do not accept his invitation (you've heard the rumors about him) but ponder its significance. You're not yet *pretty*, but your options are expanding.

So when your boyfriend's footsteps no longer echo in the stairwell, pack the essentials first: your wallet, checkbook, passport, ATM card, university I.D. Wrap your jewelry in a washcloth, what you wore from home (the ruby earrings Koko Stella told you were your mother's and the gold bangle that was your grandmother's) and even what your boyfriend gave you, because none of it was cheap. Retrieve the photographs. Count them—make sure you have all twelve. These go straight into your backpack, along with your toothbrush, two Stayfree napkins just in case, a notebook, two pens. Also pack toothpaste, shampoo, soap—one of each will do because you won't be traveling far, only to a room you've noticed advertised for rent above the Laundromat across town, on the street where Miguel's a chef in that fancy French restaurant, which is far enough.

Pack two pairs of dungarees, all your panties, four clean T-shirts and this semester's course books in your duffle bag. Leave the rest. Write a letter so your boyfriend will feel free to sell what he can and donate what remains to Goodwill.

When you leave your key on the kitchen table and shut the front door so it locks behind you, remind yourself this is all for the best.

(One day you'll know that it truly is so until then) do what others like you do, what women before you have done, what your daughter, too, may have to do—fake it. Fake it until you don't have to anymore.

Future Tense

Grace Singh Smith

Minerva missed seeing the Pacific Ocean that first time because she was asleep. When she landed at Los Angeles International Airport after twenty hours in the air, she had felt Carl's large hand on her shoulder. Wake up, wake up, we're here, we're home.

Where was the Pacific Ocean? she'd asked, disoriented, mouth dry and breath bad. He laughed at her because – while the Boeing 777 was dropping out of the clouds toward the City of Angels – her head was lolling like a string puppet not in use.

She had walked through a long corridor at the end of which President Obama's confidently friendly but distant face welcomed her to the Land of Opportunity. What a nice smile he had, and such white teeth! Then she was hit by a smell. It was more than a smell, it was a sensation – one that pricked the insides of her nostrils, and made her want to sneeze.

It was the sensation that the atmosphere she was walking into was clean, like the village shop in India with its sharp paint-like smell, which also made her nostrils tickle, but in a different way.

She remembers now how hard it was to find pure white fabric in the village. What the shopkeeper sold to you as "pure white, *safed*" always had a purple tinge to it. It was as though they were keeping the cloth ready for the brightening power of Ujala fabric whitener. Just four drops of Ujala would give your clothes the whiteness they deserve. There was, too, a picture of a woman in a dazzling white sari, and a child – also in a white dress – who popped up over the woman's shoulder like a friendly demon.

The bottle was right. Just four drops of purple liquid turned the brown water from the pond dark blue. When the white fabric that happened to be purple went into that water, it turned into white, yes, white – not blue. *What do you mean by blue?* After it dried in the sun, there would be splotches on it like purple prickly heat. But everyone called it white, and when Minerva wore such a shirt to school, the teacher said, look how nice and white her shirt is today!

But here in America, everything that is white is white. White-white.

Canoga Park.

When her fiancé Carl had written that he lived in a one-bedroom apartment in a city called Canoga Park in California, she had imagined wide streets lined by palm trees; lush green parks; beautiful blonde women with big sunglasses and flowery dresses walking on every corner; and houses with swimming pools.

Their one-bedroom apartment was on a street called Independence Avenue in Canoga Park; a little hole in a big, grey beehive with many other apartments that surrounded a patio. There was a blue swimming pool in the shape of a kidney bean around which stood a round table, a few white plastic chairs and a BBQ grill. A fake palm tree – with lights on it that glowed red and green like Christmas at night – rose into the colorless sky. The name of this apartment complex was "The Americana Independence", and when she had called and told Papa, he had been very impressed.

After they packed away all her things in the one big closet that Carl very kindly said she could have, he spent two days at home with her, taking her to a grocery store two miles away called Albertson's – where she saw more food in cans and bottles than she had ever seen in her life – and then, Carl went back to work. She was alone in her Americana Independence apartment.

The first two days, she put away all the MDH masala spices she had brought with her in small bottles, which she labeled. Then, she began to read her three Sanjeev Kapoor cookbooks to determine which dishes she could cook for Carl. She could only make those dishes that did not require too many exotic Indian ingredients. She made a list each weekend of everything she needed and Carl took her to Albertson's. At first, she followed him respectfully with the grocery cart and listened with the reverence of a churchgoer as he pointed out the difference between fat free and not, organic and not, dill pickle spears and chips, and so on. After two weeks, she knew what and where everything was, but she wanted him to feel that she relied on him. She thought maybe he wouldn't like it if she said she didn't need him to point out where things were. Until the day he got confused in the refrigerated section, looking for his Ball Park hot dogs.

Sorry, she said, as if it were her fault. Right there, under the Oscar Mayer wieners.

I knew they were there all along, he said. I wasn't paying attention.

When would she learn how to drive, she wondered. When would she go to the big Westfield Mall with endless shops that sold more things than she could ever learn to ask about or buy? Carl said that it was easy to drive but he hadn't offered to teach her. He said she should learn to read a map first and even though she had tested the highest in Geography in the state of Tripura, she had never learned how to read a map. She only memorized names of places and wrote lengthy essays about the population distribution in Europe.

A week after she arrived, Minerva had asked Carl what it was like to drive. He produced a book called *The Thomas Guide*. He said, Los Angeles is a huge city – as big as a country. It's easy to get lost and end up in the wrong neighborhood.

He showed her different squiggly lines that stood for important highways (freeways, he called them). Then, he tested her. *Which freeways will you take to get to Santa Monica?*

Her best friend in the village was a girl named Monica. She had started threading her eyebrows before anybody else, sang classical ragas and played the harmonium. And here was a city named after her friend. She thought it a good omen. She found Santa Monica on the map, and next, the 10 interstate. But somewhere in the collision of red and yellow and gray lines, she got lost. A ringing noise inside her head got loud, as Carl laughed.

She threw the book across the room. Not at him. How could she?

The thing about Ujala was that the bottle *promised* to make your clothes white. Even the TV advertisement had a promise to it: of happiness. There was the woman in the all-white sari chasing the child also-in-white, through rooms with all-white curtains fluttering, all in slow motion. Minerva had always wondered how a widow in white could be so happy. But maybe she wasn't really a widow; maybe what she was wearing was not really white but a trick of the TV. Now in America, Minerva thinks that the Ujala ad may have been a lie.

Her father had said that she could prepare a Western dinner for the son of his friend from his seminary days in the USA, who had arrived at this remote, opposite corner of the world to find purpose in life. Carl would be teaching at the local mission school for three months. Americans struggled to find true meaning in life, her father told her, because they had too much money.

She made boiled potatoes and carrots with Amul butter, and roasted chicken in the Hawkins pressure cooker. She made custard and crumbled Britannia biscuits and sliced bananas over it. Carl's eyes were green like a pond with old water but through his thick glasses, she saw a dim light. Her father looked pleased when Carl said that the food Minerva had made was the best he had ever had – since he came to India, that is.

They are complicated, these Sanjeev Kapoor recipes. Dishes she had never heard of at home in northeast India, which was not really India except in name. "Connected to the mainland by a strip of land known as the Chicken's Neck," declared geography textbooks from New Delhi. Inhabited by people referred to openly by those in the mainland as "chinkies."

Saag Wala Gosht, Paneer Jalfrezi, Khaman Dhokla…Carl calls them all simply by one name: curry. She used to find it funny. At home, she'd only cooked for fun because Papa liked to cook all their meals. Her mother had died when Minerva was seven, of typhoid. She does not remember anything except the dead body, so pretty in its red silk salwar kameez. The made-up face was a caricature of her mother, with painted eyebrows that made her look surprised and possibly about to laugh at a big joke.

Papa learned to cook. Damn anybody who made jokes about a man who cooked, try bringing back my wife from the dead, he said. People suggested maids, but he did not want to have another woman in the house. It gave the appearance of evil, he said, and as a devout Christian, he abstained from all appearance of evil.

He also washed his own clothes. Minerva never learned how Papa got exactly four drops out of the Ujala bottle. And his shirts were always

Ujala white with no splotches ever.

She has been living in the Americana Independence for six months now, and sometimes Minerva feels like it is a hotel. She doesn't know the names of any of her neighbors, even though she hears the faint buzzing of their TVs, their occasional shouting, and children crying. In India, she knew the names of all her neighbors not just in her lane, but also in the other lanes up and down the main road.

One day, as Minerva walks behind Carl after an Albertson's outing, a girl pops out of the apartment two doors down. She walks away proud as a horse, her majestically round buttocks poured into a pair of leathery black pants; and she is wearing a tube top. Minerva catches sight of it, just then. The golds, reds, and yellows of a sunset splayed on a back as expansive as the sky; giant cartoon-like ocean waves lapping her shoulders; sea gulls flying on her neck and disappearing into black hair; a bridge-like structure that goes nowhere on the left part of her upper back, with a Ferris wheel just like the kind that would come through the village in Tripura for the annual mela.

The whole magic scene is alive on the girl's olive skin.

What is that? she whispers to Carl, pointing at the receding back.

The Santa Monica Pier – a tattoo, he says, loudly.

That night, she has a dream in which the girl with the pier on her back appears. Minerva is sitting in a room full of boxes: of food, spices, and books. She wants to get up but can't; her body is heavy and she is stuck to the floor. All of a sudden, a back with a vista on it rises up like a snake, right out of an open Sanjeev Kapoor cookbook. Minerva admires the pier without fabric cutting it off. She reaches out to touch the Ferris wheel but wakes up to find herself stabbing the air with her index finger. Carl's dreadfully affectionate snoring enters her consciousness.

The train has left the station, she says out loud.

They always went everywhere together, Minerva and Papa. When she was little, she sat on his lap. She sat on his lap even up till she was fifteen or sixteen. If the bus was filled to the door with people and they had to squeeze in, her Papa shielded her from men who tried to fondle her buttocks or touch her breasts. As the bus bumped and swayed – and time lost relevance because you couldn't even look out of a window to see where you were – she felt his presence behind her, the sharp smell of Old Spice and sweat, his arms keeping her body away from danger. And now, she realizes that she never even learned how to buy a bus ticket on her own.

She asks Carl again how difficult it is to learn how to drive, as he eats a meal of chicken jhalfrezi and jeera pulao. She's also made him a side salad of iceberg lettuce, croutons and Hidden Valley bleu cheese dressing, per his request. She watches a bite of food make its way down his gullet like a knee straightening under a blanket.

LA is nuts, Carl says. I'd wait to drive if I were you, he says.

She wants to say something but her throat feels tight. She hears the crunch of his teeth on a crouton and wonders how he can possibly eat a salad – and that hideous white dressing – with Indian food. Minerva forces a smile, and heads to the kitchen to clean the stove. Indian food always leaves such a big mess and requires heavy cleaning.

The next morning – as she opens the blinds to look at the vertically sliced view of Independence Avenue and the sign of the "Thrifty Wash" opposite the Americana Independence – she decides that she will go outside for the first time. On her own, that is. Unescorted.

As she walks out of the gate of the Americana Independence, everything feels different. The air is hot. She pauses at the sidewalk, and can't decide which way she should go. She goes right but looks carefully left first. At the end of the block, there is a crosswalk. In school, she had only seen pictures of such a thing in a book, it was called a "zebra crossing". But here is a pole next to it with a metal button, and a small screen mounted on the opposite side shows a hand, which suddenly turns into numbers. She is uncertain. A man comes up beside her, running, and Minerva jumps aside. Sweat darkens a patch the shape of the African continent on his T-shirt, and he thuds on to the crosswalk without even looking at her. She plunges in behind him, and a feeling of pride swells up in her, making her smile like an idiot. When she gets to the other side, there is a gas station. "USA GAS" says the sign, declaring its allegiance. Minerva sees rows of chips, magazines with pictures of blonde women with big breasts and orange skin, and drinks behind a cold case. She fingers the quarters in her pocket and thinks she will get a soda. At home in India, the petrol pump stations did not sell anything.

HEY. A strong voice brings Minerva back to the present. It is the girl with the sunset-ocean-pier on her back.

Hello, good afternoon, Minerva says to her. My name is Minerva.

I'm Maricela, says the girl.

Marcella, repeats Minerva. The girl shakes her head, no.

Ma-ri-ce-la, the girl says, dark red lips moving over her pearl-white teeth like a serpent. She rolls the "R" like the Hindi "R."

Minerva laughs. She gets Maricela's name perfectly, then.

She is glad Maricela showed up because in the six months she has been here, she has not yet bought anything on her own. At the grocery store, she watched as Carl confidently swiped a debit card to pay for their purchases – she tried to memorize the sequence of things so she would know how to do it when the time came – but he had not yet offered to get her a debit card. When she asked him once, he inserted his index finger into her curls, and said there was no need for her to worry her pretty little head.

Maricela buys a six-pack of beer, producing cash from the back pocket of her leathery pants that cling to her body like a second skin. She stands aside, watching as Minerva timidly picks a pack of Wrigley's chewing gum. Minerva sets out four quarters, two of which the store-owner pushes back across the counter, as he points to the sign under the stack of gum that reads "50 cents." Her face feels hot.

As they walk back together, Minerva is suddenly conscious of the pavement under her feet, and gets a whiff of something like roses and candy from Maricela, who says that she always smells delicious food from Minerva's apartment. Minerva feels a balloon inflating in her chest, and says she is about to make some chicken tikka masala. Would Maricela like to taste some?

She finishes up the meal early, three hours before Carl would come home. She pours the golden curry into a Ziploc container, spoons some rice into a packet of tinfoil, and walks over to Apartment Number 19.

The apartment is painted a dark red to match Maricela's lips. There is nothing in the living room except a black leather couch and a coffee table, and no decorations on the walls save one, which has mirrors of various shapes on it. Minerva has never seen red walls or so many mirrors in one place. *Does Maricela like to look at herself?* Minerva wonders.

This is the first American person Minerva has met on her own, even though she is not white. Minerva used to think all Americans were white like Carl. Now she knows better.

After they chat a little about Indian food (Maricela promptly took it to the kitchen, where she stuck it in the freezer, to Minerva's surprise), Minerva falls silent. She is unsure of what kind of topics someone like her can discuss with someone who has a color painting on her back, wears tight trousers with no shame and buys beer like a man.

Minerva is conscious of her own brown-marble eyes, pale yellow skin, and hair almost the texture of steel wool. She feels so ordinary when she looks at Maricela, whose shiny black hair is pulled back so that Minerva can now see clearly the seagull that flies into her hairline. She sees, too, a streak of blue in Maricela's hair, like the color of water into which only four drops of Ujala has been dropped.

Maricela asks Minerva if she would like a beer. Minerva feels ashamed – Papa would be shocked if he knew she was making friends with a woman who drank alcohol – but Maricela is the first person in this country who said hello to her (other than store clerks). Minerva wonders how beer tastes: does it bubble in your mouth, make you lose your mind? She wants to ask Minerva to give her only a little, but what would Papa do?

No, thank you, she hears herself say. Only water, please, no ice.

Maricela settles next to Minerva on the couch with a brown bottle, and stretches out her long legs till her feet rest on the coffee table. Minerva asks her what she does for a living. She says she models part-time and works – also part-time – as an admin for a design studio in Santa Monica. Minerva wonders what kind of an administrator dresses in such a way and spends so many days at home. She also wants to ask what kind of design takes place in a studio, that of clothes and houses being the only kinds she is aware of. But Minerva does not want to reveal her ignorance.

Maricela tells Minerva that she really likes the green kurta she is wearing, and says it is "so cool" of Minerva to bring her some curry; and that India is on her bucket list, whatever that is.

When Minerva leaves, she smiles all the way to her door. She looks at her HMT watch and sees that they have talked for an hour and a half, and yet it seems like only twenty minutes. She scrubs the wok in which she had cooked the tikka masala with a happy feeling that she has not felt since she landed in this clean country. For the first time, a full hour goes by that she does not think of Papa.

Minerva replays their conversation in her mind as she washes the dishes. She wants to go back and talk to Maricela some more, but she understands that in this new country, people don't just drop by unannounced. Cars fly by in the street in front of her kitchen window with a last burst of speed before they roll to a stop at Parthenia Street (what a dignified name, she thinks). Rear lights flash importantly red. Usually, there is only one person inside these vehicles, and they always look very busy and preoccupied. As they wait for the light to turn, they keep glancing down at their crotch or something in it; and when the light turns green, one or two horns honk to remind the one in front to move. It makes her homesick, because at home, horns honk all the time. Po-po-po-po. She wonders if there are many people waiting for all these busy, important people wherever they are going. She wonders if they will cook a meal when they get home.

That evening when Carl walks in, Minerva has just sprinkled a handful of chopped cilantro on the golden-red meat. She now says "cilantro" instead of "coriander." Carl laughed at her the other day in the grocery store and said, *Aren't you all American now?* When he said "American," he rolled his "r" in a fake Indian accent that made her angry; she wished she had said "coriander" instead.

He greets her at the door with a forgetful kiss on the head, a squeeze on her buttocks and a comment of, *Oh, curry again!* When he walks in, his dirty-looking brown hair – neither the color of mud nor the color of an almond but somewhere in between – has flakes of white paint in it. His brown work trousers (*tan* as they like to say here in America, as if brown is a bad word) bears the proud smudges of a day's worth of work with his father's paint and drywall business, which is run out of a home office in Simi Valley. She has been there to visit twice. Once, the five employees of said business all wanted to eat an Indian breakfast. She had fried some hamburger buns in butter, and made pav bhaji with Sriracha chili sauce. *Paw bhaji*, they said and drank it all down with ugly black coffee.

Carl wears glasses. She asked him once if it was difficult to work with his hands while wearing glasses, but he gave her a look somewhere between anger and disgust, so after that she never asked him. His glasses enlarge his green eyes and when she sees through them, a slice of his face does not exist. Through the glasses, she watches his emotions as though on a movie screen. Exaggerated and magnified.

She sits opposite him at the small laminate-top table and watches him eat. She tells him that she made a friend today.

He looks surprised.

Carl says that Maricela does not seem like a "nice girl." Minerva isn't sure what he means by "nice" but he is talking in his loud voice and she doesn't feel like asking. She watches him polish off his plate as he jokes about Maricela's back and her tight pants. He makes a comment about how Hispanic women dress like *that*. Also, he says, what would that tattoo look like when she is old and everything is falling apart?

The very next morning, Minerva decides to venture outside again, on another walk. She hopes to run into Maricela. When she stands outside in the dry air of Independence Avenue, she looks right, then left.

Towards the left, all she can see are apartments, other beehives like the Americana Independence. To the right, at least there's the gas station. She turns right. No Maricela today. She walks into the gas station, picks up a magazine with a bold yellow headline: Dr. Phil Caught Cheating!

She lingers in front of the beers, and wonders if the quarters in her pocket will add up to the price of a bottle. If she were to buy one and drink it, where would she dispose of it? Would Carl smell it on her breath? Like Papa, he is a devout Christian and does not drink anything stimulating. He likes Mountain Dew, and that's all he drinks. She leaves empty-handed.

Carl walks through the screen door and says, *Curry again!* A couple flecks of white paint come floating off his head towards the tan carpet. Minerva walks away to dish out some food for him, and he asks if she would please make some salad too.

She sinks a big stainless steel spoon that she brought from India into the virginal white rice. It brings up a nice blob, filling the room with its sweet fragrance. She had mixed in a cup of jasmine for him. Would he know the difference, she wonders, and should she point it out to him? She serves him a round mound of white rice perfectly shaped in a bowl and then overturned; a bowl of chicken curry; a plate of cucumbers, tomatoes and lettuce; and on the side, bleu cheese dressing.

He eats it all noisily in their dining area, as she watches.

Papa did not like for her to go outside alone. Because you are beautiful, he said, and boys will come after you; they will kidnap you, and make you sleep with them and then you will have to marry them. So, she only left the house with him, and they rode the bus together: to school and to the town fifteen miles away and anywhere in between. Wherever the road ran.

One day, after that first dinner, Carl came by for tea before they all went to their New Life Fellowship Church, and Papa happened to be in the bathroom. It was the first time she had been alone with another man. When she handed him a cup of tea, her fingers brushed his; a shock pierced her belly, and went out through her toes. At the end of his three months, many dinners, many cups of tea, and many church services – in which he sat in the pew directly in front of her – Carl approached her father to ask if he could "court" Minerva. She had listened behind the wall, and was in awe that he had used the word "court," it made her feel like a heroine in olden times. A year and many phone conversations later, he returned to ask Papa for Minerva's hand in marriage. Papa asked Minerva to pray about it but she saw the smile on his face. She had never felt like this before. There were only two eligible Christian boys in her church: one was uneducated, the other had bad breath and chewed paan. Papa had told her such wonderful stories about America, too, and who knew what she might become in the Land of Opportunity? The shirts Carl wore – unbuttoned at the top – were pure white. His breath smelled like pudina and new milk. She decided yes.

One week and three days after her first walk outside, she sees Maricela when she steps out to read her devotional *Our Daily Bread* in a chair by the kidney-bean pool. Minerva hesitates, and then invites Maricela to their apartment for a cup of tea. The teacups will be washed by the time Carl gets home, and he does not have to know.

A number of white threads from her torn denim shorts dangle over Maricela's bronzed legs and she is wearing a top with too-large holes for the arms. Minerva makes tea with elaichi, bay leaves and cloves. Maricela says it's the best tea she has ever had.

Chai, Minerva says.

Chai, Maricela repeats like a tape recorder.

Minerva asks Maricela about her parents, and Maricela says she does not know who her father is or where he is. Her mother lives in Arizona. Minerva tells her about Papa and how he took care of her, and Maricela looks away, but not in an unfriendly way. They talk and talk, and after the first ten minutes, Minerva forgets to look at the wall clock.

Finally, Maricela says, You wanna come with me to Santa Monica one of these days? I *love* the beach…we could just hang out…it's such a happy place.

Just then, Minerva jumps up, because Carl's shadow is visible through the blinds of the lone front window. The door creaks angrily as he walks in. His green eyes look cloudy, and his brows crowd in towards each other.

Hi, he says to Maricela. It is the shortest sentence. He walks into the kitchen and they hear the fridge door slam, and then the abrupt pop of a soda can.

What are we eating for dinner? he asks, loudly, without appearing. As if Maricela isn't even there. Maricela sets her cup on the table.

Sorry, she says, and leaves.

Last night, Minerva had called Papa from Carl's mobile phone using an African Queen calling card. He asked her if she had found any Ujala to make sure Carl's white shirts stayed really white. She had laughed at him and reminded him that here, they washed all their clothes in a laundromat in the building, where all the whites got washed with bleach and came out real white, not fake white.

There was silence on the line and she saw Carl gesturing to have his phone back, so she said, Papa? His small, distant voice said, Be a good girl, take good care of Carl. Then: a beep and a hum.

They fight. Carl says he does not like having a woman like Maricela in his home. She cries and says, I have nothing to do, no friends, I am nothing…I am just a housewife and I don't even have a car to go anywhere.

Later that night, she feels Carl's hands reaching for her – they make love on a bi-weekly basis, when he is not tired from working sixty hours a week – and he claims her, in a way more tender than usual. She is glad that it is dark because she is staring at the ceiling, wishing she were somewhere else instead of here. Maybe back home with Papa, maybe not. Maybe at the beach in Santa Monica.

For three days, she does not step outside the apartment. She sleeps till two in the afternoon; and then wakes up to dust the furniture, scrub the toilet and make dinner for Carl. On the fourth day, as they eat dinner in silence, Carl says that his father has an older but well-functioning 1990 Toyota Corolla, and he says that Minerva can have it.

She does not look up from her stainless steel plate but through the rice and curry, she sees her own face. She sees hope.

Wow, wow, wow, says Papa on the phone. What a lucky girl you are!

It is second-hand, Papa.

Second-hand? Don't forget we only rode buses! Be very grateful, child…what a wonderful husband you have. God bless you both.

That night, Minerva has a dream in which she is washing Carl's shirts in a bucket of water with only four drops of Ujala in it. When she pulls them out, they come out perfectly white – American white-white, not Ujala Indian blue-white. She wonders what would happen if she put in six – no, seven drops. Plop, plop, plop, plop, plop, plop, plop. Minerva drowns one of his perfect white shirts in the purple water. It emerges spotty like a leper's face rendered in purple. She wakes up laughing.

The Toyota Corolla is beautiful, although it has a dent and the seats have towels stretched across for covers. Carl appears to have some doubts about her readiness to drive – he pulls out *The Thomas Guide* again and quizzes her on her knowledge of the local streets – and she cries for an hour after he falls asleep, exactly ten minutes after he had changed into his ridiculous Charlie Brown pajamas.

While she is learning how to drive, she does not see Maricela often. One afternoon, Minerva heads out to the gas station to buy Circus Peanuts, and she runs into Maricela, who is striding out her door with a duffle bag.

Nice to see you, Minerva says.

Maricela looks sad.

One of these days, she says, when you're free, we can have fun together. She says "free" as if she is talking about the Quit India movement. She leaves right then, as if she knows that Minerva is struggling with the question of how to tell her that she wants to invite her for a cup of tea but can't. Maricela says goodbye – or just bye? – so fast that Minerva is not sure she heard it at all.

It takes her one month with the Dollar Training School, and three failed tests at the Department of Motor Vehicles, which almost reminds her of an Indian bank with its long lines and bored clerks. And then, one day – one day – she pulls over in a gray driveway and an old DMV employee with a long braid looks over his checklist and shakes her hand. You passed, he says, his 'a' coming through the nose.

Great, Carl says, with a small smile. Now you can go to the grocery store on your own.

Minerva asks Carl if they could go to Santa Monica beach. She has never been to a beach or seen the ocean, but he says that he really hates traffic on the 405 and the 10. What is the hurry, he says, since she lives in LA now? Someday, when he has more time, they will go. It is too crowded of a place and just overrated, he says.

She knows she will never ask him again.

Minerva only drives the car to the grocery store two miles away and she carries cash with her, fifty dollars. She carefully reads all the labels, and adds the prices as she goes along to not go over her budget. Carl claps her on the back when he gets home every Wednesday and says what an American she is turning out to be. She does not know how to pump gas and since she doesn't drive anywhere else, he fills the gas tank for her every three weeks.

A month after her first drive – as she cruises along at thirty miles per hour to Albertson's – she looks at the freeway sign for the 101 South leading to Santa Monica, and she wonders if she can do it. She turns on the left indicator and segues into the left lane. A half-minute before she would curve upward to join the roaring traffic, she returns right.

Her Papa had told her that she must always obey her husband, just like she obeyed him. A good girl, raised right, obeyed her elders; and when she was married, her husband. If she didn't do so, it meant that she did not love her elders and also that she had not been raised right.

Now she washes all Carl's white shirts in a machine with bleach.

And she even has her own car. But she wants to be busy, too, and go places where there will be other people waiting for her. Albertson's is such a small store once you get used to it. She no longer has to look at the signs in the aisles to know which one for beans and rice, which one for the readymade Hamburger Helpers and DiGiorno pizza, with the fat crust Carl likes.

On a day like any other except that Minerva stays in bed thirty minutes past two, Maricela leaves the Americana Independence.

She has a new boyfriend, she says, and he asked her to live with him in his apartment in Santa Monica. Minerva feels helpless, she feels as though she should stop Maricela from making this big mistake – from living in sin – but no words come. She does not know how true they would sound anyway.

Here, Maricela says, shoving a piece of paper at Minerva. Here's my address and number…come visit me sometime, now that you're driving and everything. She plants a kiss on Minerva's left cheek. It feels as if a butterfly has entered Minerva's skin.

When she walks away, the sunset on her back glows in the ordinary beige light of the Americana Independence like a goddess's avatar come to unworthy human earth. The vision disappears in front of Minerva's eyes.

That evening, Minerva makes Carl a Hamburger Helper meal. She has gained a quick familiarity with the ready-made meals available at Albertson's with the most appetizing pictures on the boxes. At dinner, she is not hungry.

I want to work, she says. I have an MA in Geography.

He looks at her, stops eating, and takes off his glasses, as though that could help him see her better.

And now I can drive, she adds.

Carl says that she should be grateful she does not need anything. That he works fifty hours a week and overtime, so that she can stay at home and be comfortable, go for walks or read or whatever. She reminds him that she had been a part-time teacher at a high school in Tripura, and that it only takes her two hours during the day to cook, clean, scrub the toilet, and take care of their three potted tomato plants.

I can drive now, she says, again and again.

And where exactly do you go? he says, in a tone she would have used to ask her students in India where the Himalayas were.

He repeats the question, and begins to laugh, because he thinks that she is about to laugh too. In reality, she is trying not to cry. No, she decides, this time she will not cry. She will drive. And she will not go to Albertson's.

When she walks out, grabbing her car keys, Carl does not stop her because he thinks she is putting on a show. He keeps eating brown Hamburger Helper.

She pulls out *The Thomas Guide* from inside the glove compartment, and copies down the directions to Santa Monica Beach on the back of a receipt from Albertson's. 101 South, 405 South, 10 West. She memorizes them.

As she guides the Toyota Corolla into humming flight on to the freeway, no fear – no fear – fills her, just a feeling of being headed where everyone else is. The vibration of cars flying past her…the red of the brake lights glowing like fireflies…the heat in her head…the growing warmth in her hands…the emptiness in her heart… Santa

Monica Beach is just ahead, she tells herself. A place Maricela said was a happy place. Minerva wishes she had a mobile phone so she could call Maricela when she gets there. She will see if she can find her on the beach.

Finally, she comes to a street called Ocean. She sees the Pacific Ocean for the very first time in the distance, like a wall of grey-blue glass that will come crashing down on the world any minute. The sun carves a tunnel of orange light through it. It makes her want to weep.

She drives along very slowly, taking in the palm trees, people on a wide path with their legs slicing confidently back and forth on rollerblades. She sees many women wearing flimsy clothing and who don't look ashamed of it at all. She pulls over to a curb but realizes that she is not sure where to park or how to pay for parking. At Albertson's, she just parks in a lot and she has never operated a parking meter. She pulls away and as she turns a corner, she sees the pier stretched out into the ocean, a magical accident.

The sky turns a dark blue as if too many drops of Ujala have fallen in, then orange just like on Maricela's back. The Ferris wheel at the end of the pier glows like a never-ending smile. Minerva wishes again that she had a mobile phone, that she knew where and how to park; because if she did, she would walk onto that pier, and get on the Ferris wheel.

Then, she would look out, and watch the sun set over the mighty Pacific, as it rose over her Papa where he was washing his shirts to get them white. Ujala-white.

Maybe even Maricela is waiting there.

Four Suitcases

Ani Kazarian

At five years old, Armen would say, "I want," and Karena would complete the sentence with, "chicken and rice." To them, being born three days less than a year apart was equivalent to having been born on the same day. They were twins. The kind of twins that live in unison, but just happen to be two distinct entities, like the right and left arms of one body. They shared the stepstool in the bathroom while brushing their teeth, her left foot and Armen's right, the other dangling from either side as they leaned against the sink. *Good digestion starts with the teeth*, they had heard somewhere and repeated nightly.

They would watch cartoons in the morning before school, and *The Three Stooges* in the evening before bed. Once the old man let them stay up after the Stooges to watch a movie about the Wild West in America. He never let that happen again after the twins cut strips from the bottom of Loosi's lace curtains to use as rope and hogtie their stuffed animals.

One Saturday night, they particularly enjoyed watching an episode with the Stooges sawing away at a wooden object. The next morning the twins awoke at dawn. Armen climbed up the counter and brought down the cereal while Karena waited with the milk in hand. They shared one large yellow bowl with two spoons to enjoy their favorite breakfast: sweetened cereal flakes with feta cheese. One of their own creations.

After they had finished breakfast and placed the dishes in the sink,

Armen pushed the stool under the drawer beside the old gas stove. Karena climbed up to get the bread knife. They tiptoed across the vinyl kitchen floor and into the dining room. They could hardly contain their excitement, stopping regularly to cover their mouths with their hands as they giggled. They were afraid of waking the old man, but their excitement was too great for either to really think about anything other than the project at hand.

They took hold of one of the dining chairs and laid it down on the floor. They sat opposite each other with the chair between them. Karena held onto one end of the bread knife and Armen the other. She pulled as he pushed and they continued from there, back and forth with swift movements they sawed away. Just like the Stooges. One leg followed by another, done with one chair and moving on to the next. They were making good time. After sawing the legs off all the chairs, they put them back together, delicately balancing the seats on the sawed off legs so that no one would be able to tell.

Karena looked to Armen and rubbed her hands together, imagining herself as one of the villains from their morning cartoons. *I'm only missing the mustache,* she thought. Armen sat with his legs folded under him, biting his bottom lip and wiggling from left to right as he often did when excited and impatient. Side by side they sat in front of the TV, watching Sunday morning cartoons and awaiting their unsuspecting victim.

Loosi walked out from the bedroom. Armen and Karena had secretly hoped that the old man would have been first to fall prey to their trap. Loosi would have to do, an innocent victim of inopportune timing. Armen and Karena winked at each other and shouted a mischievous "Good morning." Loosi shot them a quick glance, but quickly busied herself in the kitchen, preparing tea, putting away the dishes from the night before, softly singing to herself off-key.

Their hearts beat quickly in their chests. Armen continued to wiggle from side to side, his entire body wagging like the tail of a giant dog. Karena felt her ears turning red; the excitement was too much. *It's too much,* she wanted to shout.

Finally, as Loosi began setting the table for breakfast, she reached for one of the dining room chairs and tried to pull it out. She found herself holding the backrest while the crooked remnants of the oak-stained wooden chair lay scattered across the grey carpet. Armen and Karena heard the commotion, but didn't turn around. They giggled quietly to themselves. Loosi tried another chair and then another. Armen and Karena lost the ability to control their laughter.

"Armen, Karena!" Loosi yelled, more like it was one word than two names. For such a gentle creature, her scream was gut wrenching. A moment later, the old man shuffled into the hall from the bedroom in his striped pajama bottoms and white undershirt. He stood between the living room and the dining room, saw the mess, and quickly scanned the room to rest his eyes on the twins. He turned back into the bedroom and rushed out again holding the leather belt.

Armen and Karena exchanged a quick glance of panic before running to hide behind the couch's brown cushioned comfort, wishing they could disappear into the white plastered walls like the smoke from the old man's cigarettes. He pulled the couch away from the wall and they screamed as they held onto each other. Loosi ran up to the old man from behind and grabbed his arm, pleading for him to leave the children alone. The old man pushed her back with an effortless shove. Loosi stumbled, tripped over her light pink nightgown, and hit the floor. Armen and Karena ran down the hall and into the bedroom. They shut the door and jumped on the bed to hide. The old man barged in and pulled the cover off the twins, the belt lashing down. Armen threw a pillow over Karena and took the lashes for the two of them. Karena screamed and cried as she tried to get out from under Armen. Armen remained silent, not once wincing from the pain. Loosi begged for it to stop while hitting the old man with her slipper. Eventually, he tired and walked away lighting a cigarette. His first inhale was long and deep, as if relaxing after accomplishing a great feat.

Karena lay on the tear-stained blankets. Armen lay with his eyes open, staring blankly at the wall in front of him, the lashes on his back swollen and throbbing. Loosi sat on the edge of the bed with her head in her hands. No one moved, as though everything would be different if they remained motionless long enough. Eventually Loosi stood and walked out, shutting the door softly behind her. Karena peeked her head out from the covers and saw Armen, his wounded back, his black hair forming an upside-down mountain top as it peaked perfectly at the nape of his neck. At times Karena would longingly watch Armen, as though their time together was limited. She admired his unique grace. His black eyelashes extending long and thick, creating an outline for his large eyes in likeness to the drawings of Armenia's ancient kings.

"Armen?" she whispered.

There was no response.

The world of that tiny bedroom was frozen in white plastered loneliness. She could feel Armen's anger, a silent bitterness growing in him.

Karena covered her head with the blanket and lay motionless. She drifted off to sleep, but must have had a nightmare. She woke up from the sound of her own screams, sweating.

Loosi rushed into the room. "What's happened?" She swooped Karena into her arms, resting her head against her chest. Armen rose quietly and walked over to crawl into the space between their mama and the edge of the bed.

Karena tried to tell Loosi that she had had a dream, but couldn't remember what it was about. Loosi stroked her dark hair and gently kissed Armen's forehead as she told the story of how the wise words es *el ge ansanee* came about.

It was the Shah of ancient Persia who summoned a highly celebrated poet and asked him to create one verse—one sentence that would hold true under any circumstance—and could devotedly be applied to every emotion. The poet returned with these words, *es el ge ansanee*, and was banished from the palace. On his deathbed, the Shah asked the poet to grace the palace with his presence once again. *This too shall pass.*

Loosi and the twins cuddled together on the bed, telling stories and laughing softly. The rest of the day passed uneventfully, and they were able to sleep that night without interruption. The old man did not sleep. He sat on the floor in the corner of the living room smoking cigarettes and drinking tea.

The following morning, Armen had a sore throat. It wasn't the first time he'd woken up with bright red tonsils, unable to swallow and preferring not to speak. Loosi kept him home from school and on a strict diet of rice and yogurt. She was glad that she had remembered her mother's recipe since the only yogurt in Germany came with fruit. She was sure that no one in Iran would believe that people ate their yogurt sweet.

The first morning that Armen was back to his full strength, Loosi made waffles for breakfast, a treat she usually reserved for weekends. The twins ate greedily then prepared for school. Karena helped Armen tie his shoes and zip up his jacket. Sometimes he had a hard time completing small tasks with his hands. Bundled in scarves and thick coats, the twins held hands and walked beside Loosi. They enjoyed their walk to school along the Pader River, its thick gray water gurgling over rocks and branches. Autumn in Paderborn was cold and gloomy in a way that seemed to fill the world with a lingering fog, as though each day existed only in a dream.

The twins were admiring the river when Loosi suddenly came between them and grabbed each one by the arm. She quickened her pace and they struggled to keep up. Something hard hit Karena on the crown of her head. She stopped to look up, expecting something had fallen from one of the trees. Loosi pulled Karena's arm and dragged her along, not letting her stop. There were footsteps behind them.

"Hurry." Loosi's scream was frightening, her grip twisting their wrists.

"Hunde." A man shouted from behind. "Run away dogs!" There were three men chasing Loosi and the twins. They wore black with chains dangling from their pockets and had long colorful hair that stood up above their heads.

"We'll throw your children in the river!" They threw a few more rocks.

"Run! Run!" Loosi was breathing heavily. The twins tried to keep up but the cold air hurt to breathe.

"Filthy Arabs," the men shouted.

The footsteps behind them stopped. They could hear the men laughing. The chase lasted less than a minute, but Loosi and the twins ran the rest of the way to school. Karena lost her scarf somewhere along the way.

"They didn't mean any harm," Loosi said once they reached the school and had stopped long enough to catch their breaths. "I think they were still drunk from last night." The twins nodded in agreement, as though they understood.

"Are we Arab, Mama?" Karena asked.

"No. We're Armenian. You know that." Loosi said. "Go in now, you'll be late for school."

"Why did they call us Arab?" Karena wasn't sure what Arab meant.

"They must have thought that's what we are." Loosi was growing impatient.

"Is that why they threw rocks?"

"No. They just didn't know what they were doing."

Loosi hugged them longer than she normally did. She squeezed the back of Armen's neck as though she needed to be sure that he was still there. He hadn't spoken since they started running.

"What's your name?" Mrs. Shultz asked with an anticipatory smile while parents and other teachers looked on. Armen and Karena stood at the center of the circle of teachers and parents holding hands, Armen's right leg crossed over his left as he peered out at the women.

"Schön Karena," Karena said. All the women laughed. She had learned that most people loved hearing her say it, and asked regularly just to hear it again.

Mrs. Shultz laughed with her whole body and ran her veiny hand down Karena's black hair, repeating the word *schön, schön.* Beautiful. The Germans often told Karena and Armen that their black hair was beautiful. For some time Karena believed that *schön* preceded her name. *Schön Karena.*

Loosi stood outside of the circle until the twins saw her and she nudged her way toward them. She nodded a greeting to Mrs. Shultz and the crowd slowly dispersed.

"How was school today?" Loosi asked as the three of them made their way back to the apartment.

"We danced," Karena said.

Each day their teachers walked the class upstairs to the attic with a slanted ceiling and lots of windows that trickled in the pale sunlight. There was a wall of cubbyholes where all the students housed their dance shoes. Karena's were made of red canvas with a picture of a mouse printed on the toe of each shoe. They'd change their shoes, form a circle, and dance to Mrs. Shultz singing German folk songs while the assistant teacher jingled the tambourine. It was Karena's favorite part of the day.

"What about your day, Armen?" Loosi looked down at him.

Armen shrugged his shoulders. He didn't like dancing or his blue plaid dance shoes.

"I think you need a haircut, Armen. Let's get you a real one this time." Loosi led them into a salon. It was the first time the twins had been in a salon. The hairdresser was a round woman with short blond hair and a big smile. Loosi asked for a haircut in her broken German and pointed to Armen. The woman sat him down on a tall leather chair in front of the mirror. There was a poster on the wall of a teenager with his blond hair spiked out.

"I want you to make my hair that color," Armen said to the hairdresser.

She chuckled. "You're too young now. Come back in ten years and I'll do it for you."

Armen watched himself in the mirror as she cut his hair.

After dinner, while Loosi was cleaning up the kitchen and the old man was still watching TV, the twins decided to play in the other room instead of watching the Stooges. Loosi didn't think anything of it until she noticed that they had been too quiet for too long. She followed their whispers into the bathroom and gasped at the sight of the twins.

"We're playing hairdresser, Mama." Armen smiled.

"Do you like it?" Karena turned her head to model her new cut. They had taken Karena's red plastic chair into the bathroom and placed it in front of the mirror. Karena sat down while Armen draped a bed sheet over her shoulders and took up the little plastic scissors that had been part of a gift.

"What would you like today?" Armen had asked in German.

"Make my hair like yours," Karena said.

It had taken Armen sometime to cut through Karena's long thick hair with those plastic scissors, but he had done it. Her cut was uneven, alternating between one to two inches in length. The twins giggled and Karena couldn't stop admiring herself in the mirror.

"Just clean up that hair and go to bed." Loosi shook her head and walked out of the bathroom. She held back from yelling at them because she wanted to delay the old man finding out.

The following morning, Mrs. Shultz was standing outside of the building with another parent when Loosi and the twins reached the school. Loosi waved hello and bent down to say goodbye to the twins.

"Why did you do that to her hair?" Mrs. Shultz approached them.

"The kids were just playing together," Loosi said.

"It's so crooked." Mrs. Shultz touched Karena's short strands and gave Loosi a look of horror.

"Isn't it schön?" Karena asked. She and Armen giggled.

Loosi went out that evening and returned with an envelope in her hands. She brought the aroma of autumn into the apartment and Karena could feel the chilled wind wrapped around Loosi's blue coat. She loved the smell of the cold: the scent of her mother coming home. Karena reached up and wrapped her arms around Loosi's thighs, shoveling her face into the deep blue coat to swim in that familiar fragrance. Loosi didn't seem to notice Karena clinging to her, nor did she comment on Armen's unresponsiveness. Loosi's eyes were fixed on the envelope as she slipped her index finger between its lips and tore it open. The letter was in English and Loosi used the little she knew of that language to decipher the contents.

"We're going to America."

Armen pulled himself away from the TV, and walked over to Loosi. The twins weren't exactly sure what that meant, but knew that it was what they had been waiting for as far back as either could remember. They jumped up and down, circling Loosi and cheering. Loosi made her way toward the phone with slow mechanical steps. It used to be all Loosi and the old man talked about.

Armen walked after her and pushed his hand into her palm. Loosi paused and look down. His physical affection was so rare that he had her full attention.

"Mama, when we go to America, can you, Karena, and I live together without Sombat?"

"Armen? You don't want to live with Sombat?" Loosi asked, though she knew he didn't want to live with the old man. She didn't want to live with him either. "He's your father."

Armen stood with his head slightly tilted to the left as his eyes stared into Loosi's.

Loosi didn't know what to say without disappointing him so she removed his hand from hers, picked up the receiver, and dialed the numbers on the calling card.

"We just got the letter. We only have three days. Looks like we'll see you at the airport on Thursday," Loosi said. She didn't sound excited. "After four years of waiting to go to America, they give us three days to get ready."

"I want to talk to him. I want to talk to him," Karena knew Loosi had called their Uncle Martik in America because she was speaking very loudly.

Loosi handed her the phone.

"Hi Uncle Martik. We're going to see you. We can play and eat American cheeseburgers together." Karena spoke with giggles between each of her words.

"Don't trouble your mom on the way over." Uncle Martik sounded very far away.

Armen and Karena imagined him to be an old man with a long

white beard, even though they knew he was younger than their mother. Karena turned to look at Armen and Loosi, expecting something big to happen. Loosi went into the kitchen and started peeling potatoes.

"Mama. What are you doing?"

"I'm making dinner. What does it look like I'm doing?"

"But what about America?" Karena started to fear that it wasn't real.

"We know we're going to America, but what am I supposed to do about it now?"

Disappointed, Karena returned to the living room and started a game of being a bank teller behind a cardboard teller window waiting for Armen, the dangerous outlaw, to rob her with his cowboy gun.

Armen and Karena were almost done setting the table when the old man walked in through the front door. "Is dinner ready?"

"Sosik. Sosik. We're going to America," Karena shouted as she ran toward him with her arms stretched open, anticipating a hug.

Loosi sighed.

"What is she saying?" he walked past Karena.

She lifted her open arms and spun around like a ballerina. The old man's smell of cigarettes and beer lingered in the air as he walked toward the kitchen. Armen didn't move.

"Tell me what is going on?"

"The letter came. It's here on the counter," Loosi said.

Sombat nodded to himself as he read the letter. He folded it several times until it was a small square, and placed it in his shirt pocket. His pace was hurried. He took long heavy strides down the hall. The twins looked up, but didn't move when they heard the sound of things being thrown around in the bedroom.

"Dinner is ready." Loosi placed a steaming plate of rice and potatoes on the table.

After dinner, the old man rummaged through the house without a shirt on, breaking the bookshelf and potted plants. "We don't have any time," he shouted.

"What are you doing?" Loosi stood in the center of the living room with shreds of paper, empty boxes, and furniture scattered across the floor. The twins stood behind her. Neither of them understood why everything needed to be destroyed.

"We can't take it with us. We're leaving anything that doesn't fit in those four suitcases." Sombat ripped up the bed sheets and a stuffed animal.

Karena cried at the sight of her koala missing an arm. Armen put his arm around her shoulders. "Es el ge ansanee," he said.

Strange Leaves

Christopher Carmona

#immigrationshuffle

Steps off of bus. Downtown McAllen. After surrendering to Border Patrol. Given ticket to see judge in 3-6 months. Options are simple: take bus ride to detention center deep in U.S. territory or report to refugee center located 2 blocks south of bus station. Shī barely understands since only knows few words English and not much more Spanish. Shī mostly speaks Quecha. Shī mostly gestures and points on Border Patrol paper map. Shī points at church. Symbol she knows well. Cruz blanco...white cross...salvation she hopes. Shī walks down city block filled with tiendas, parking garages, and loud blasting norteño music. Streets are different yet same somehow. Many brown faces. A few white ones but not too many. Shī was expecting English but this place is more Spanish. More Mexican. Maybe I'm not in America yet, she thinks. But keeps walking to church. Shī goes to first building that looks like church. It is white with big wooden cross on steeple. Has to be it, she thinks. Tries door. It is locked. Hears footsteps. Older woman with glasses answers door. Opens it just a bit, enough for half her face.

"Can I help you?" woman says.

"No hablo ingles. Habla español?" Shī asks.

"Si, mija. ¿Que quieres?"

"Estoy buscando Say-cri-ed Heart."

"¿Usted es inmigrante, mija?"

Shī nods head while woman explains where to go. Strange, she thinks, she never opened door all the way. Just enough for her to talk. Then shut it hard and fast. Walks past two buildings until she rounds corner and sees six big tents with giant air conditioners making its plastic walls shake. Red Cross truck sits just past gate. TV news vans with names like Telemundo, Galavision, and Univision are at door where woman with blue vest tells her to go in. Woman in blue vest never gets off phone. Everyone speaks Spanish here. Shī walks into building where women with blue vests are everywhere. Clothes in piles. Tables with food. Tables with toothpaste, brushes, and deodorants. No one says anything to her at first but then young girl with hair in bun walks up and says, "Hola. ¿Puedo ayudarle?"

Shī explains her story to girl. Long walks in desert. Riding on top of trains. Same shoes. Same clothes. Same everything for days. Girl with hair in bun tells her many things, some she doesn't understand. Shī knows Spanish but only a little. When she attempts to tell girl with bun in hair that she doesn't speak Spanish well, girl cuts her off. Girl with hair in bun shows her to room with small shower and plastic curtain. Shī smiles for first time in weeks. Girl in bun tells her that she will have new clothes when she is done. Shī smiles again. Shī takes shower and sees new clothes on chair waiting for her. Shī puts on new clothes. Feels like new person. No longer dirty. No longer Shi. Girl in bun comes around corner and asks, "why no bra and panties?"

Look comes over her face that takes her back to the Shī she was before shower. Shī looks at girl with hair in bun and tells her that coyotes made her hang them from tree after… Girl in bun looks horrified. Becomes speechless. Shī looks at girl and steps closer and tells her that it is okay. Shī smiles again because she took pill before. No baby.

#rapetreesarereal
iTELEGRAM

Haldon Cruces [Donna, TX] to Rowena Garza [Albquerque, NM]

Message:
I heard a strange sound when I was on the road {stop} It was night and I was somewhere around King Ranch {stop} I was definitely south of Sarita checkpoint. {stop} Had pulled over to take a piss and thought I heard a woman scream {stop} Didn't know exactly what it was {stop} At first I thought it was a coyote or maybe a goat {stop} but deep down I knew it was something horrible {stop} I contemplated whether I should check it out {stop} My conscience told me that I had to check, so I did. {stop} I zipped up and turned on the flashlight app. {stop} At first I thought I saw the shadow of three people run across the darkened brush {stop} Maybe it was the ghosts of immigrants that never quite made it {stop} But I knew better. {stop} Walked up to the barbed wire fence. {stop} I knew it was ranch land and private property but the sounds of a woman crying forced me to trespass. {stop} What I saw, bro, was worse than anything I could have imagined. {stop} First I saw a tree with strange leaves {stop} The woman was lying on the ground wearing only a shirt {stop} No pants, no panties, just a pair of sandals and a white shirt with a pink ribbon on it {stop} The shirt read, Help End Breast Cancer. {stop} Don't know why that is important, but it is {stop} She looked at me and told me in Spanish {stop} "Leave me before they come back and kill you." {stop} I told her in my best broken Spanish that I had a car and I could take her where she needed to go {stop} She looked at me, not ready to trust me {stop} She hung her bra and panties from a tree and said {stop} She couldn't go with me because the coyotes would find her and kill her {stop} I explained that this is America and the Border Patrol are only a few miles up the road {stop} "We can make it,"

I told her. {stop} She agreed and she followed me back to my car. {stop} I turned to look one last time {stop} Too many bras. Too many panties. Too many strange leaves {stop} My heart was pounding waiting for the coyotes to jump out and kill us {stop} But that never happened, she got in my car {stop} I told her my name and asked hers {stop} She told me her name was Shi, I didn't argue {stop} We sped down the road to the checkpoint and I pulled over {stop} I did something I have never done and flagged down the first BP I could find {stop} I told him my story and at first he didn't believe me {stop} But then when she corroborated the story they took her inside the station {stop} I was there 3 hours before they let me go {stop} I asked what was going to happen to her {stop} BP guy told me that she was going to be processed and probably let go {stop} I couldn't believe my ears {stop} I thought for sure they would deport her {stop} BP guy told me no because she was the victim of a crime {stop} she gets a special visa and gets to see a judge {stop} Crazy right? I didn't know {stop} I got to speak to her one last time, then I gave her my card {stop} told her I lived in McAllen and if she needed anything {stop} Don't know if I will ever see her again {stop} I did my good deed for the day {stop} Catch you later bro, write back as soon as you get this {stop}

#roadisalwaysbumpyanddark

Shī doesn't know what to do. Road is bumpy. Back of van is backed so tight, legs are starting to cramp from not being able to move. Shī closes her eyes and hopes ride is almost over. How many in here, she asks herself. Too many, she answers. Maybe ten, maybe more. Shī is only young girl by herself in this van. Others are mother and grandmother's age. Shī was sent alone. Mother didn't want her back home. Shī was fourteen about to be fifteen. Men on streets back in Guatemala starting to notice growing breasts on chest. Ass being shaped by growing hips. Thinning face and fuller lips. Mother tells her she is becoming a woman now. Shī thought she was woman when turned 13 she bled for first time. Men didn't look at her then. Now body aging faster than mind. Now Shī is woman.

Shī looks around darkened van. No real seats. No windows. Just smell of people sardined. At first, it bothered her. Now, she doesn't even smell anymore. Other groups almost all made up of kids her age. This group is mostly grandfathers, mothers without children, and young men with fear in eyes and hope in heart. One woman asks if she is scared. Shī thinks it is strange question. Aren't we all? she replies. Woman whose name is Benita Gomez-Santander touches her shoulder and smiles. Smile is most distraught she has ever seen.

"No," she says, "Are you scared of these men?"

Shī has not really thought of it. She knew what the unspoken penalty was going to be, so she puts thought out of mind. For sanity. Shī asks Benita, "Are you scared?"

Benita looks at her and smiles again. This time the way a mother looks at daughter knowing that something terrible is coming and she can't stop or protect her. "Mijita," Benita says, "This isn't my first ride."

Shī just looks down and Benita just holds her until van stops and sound of car doors opening and closing is heard. Benita then puts something in her hand and says, "Take this."

Shī is confused and doesn't react, so Benita looks her dead in eye and says, "Take it, por favor, now!"

Shī only has swallow left of water and so she does as Benita asked. She swallows pill. Tastes bitter. Benita hugs one last time and says, "No baby. Not for you."

She feels hot tear trickle down Benita's cheek and onto her forehead.

#refugeegirlatmydoorstep

Rowena Garza: Yeah?

Haldon Cruces: Dude, I need your help.

Rowena: What's going on, man?

Haldon: You remember that telegram I sent you about the girl I rescued?

Rowena: Yeah, that was weird.

Haldon: Well, she's here.

Rowena: Wait, what do you mean she's there?

Haldon: She's here at my house.

Rowena: How'd she find you?

Haldon: I gave her my card.

Rowena: Why'd you do that?

Haldon: I don't know. I just did.

Rowena: Well now she's your problem.

Haldon: Thanks, I know that.

Rowena: How old is she?

Haldon: I don't know, thirteen maybe. Why?

Rowena: Because you're a thirty-five year old man, recently divorced, with an underage immigrant girl in your apartment.

Haldon: Dude, I'm not a pedophile. She's a kid.

Rowena: And stop calling me dude. I'm a woman now. Doesn't my voice sound silky smooth like Angelina Jolie in Salt?

Haldon: Rowena, I know you're a woman now. But you sound more like Harvey Firestone in Mrs. Doubtfire.

Rowena: FU, you just jealous.

Haldon: Rowena, can we focus on one problem at a time here?

Rowena: Alright, Hal, honey. Is there a social worker you can call?

Haldon: The social worker dropped her off here.

Rowena: The social worker drove her to your house? Why would they do that?

Haldon: Because all she had on her was my business card.

Rowena: Why would you put your home address on your business card anyway? You're a writer. There are a lot of Misery creeps out there.

Haldon: Rowena focus.

Rowena: Alright already. Tell the social worker you can't take her in.

Haldon: I did that already. Vanessa told me she had nowhere else to go. She has no family here.

Rowena: Whose Vanessa?

Haldon: The social worker.

Rowena: Oh okay. Ummm….I don't know, honey. You are in uncharted territory here. What are the girl's options?

Haldon: Going to a detention center somewhere deep in the Midwest or…

Rowena: Or what?

Haldon: Staying here.

Rowena: You want to take care of this girl, don't you?

Haldon: I don't know.

Rowena: I hear it in your voice. She is not your problem. You did more than anyone can expect. You rescued that girl.

Haldon: But I feel responsible for her.

Rowena: Oh Hal. You and your conscience. They always get you in trouble.

Haldon: What do I do?

Rowena: You already took her in, didn't you?

Haldon: [silence]…yes I did.

Rowena: Then why you calling?

Haldon: You know why?

Rowena: I'm your friend, not your mother or your wife. You don't need my permission.

Haldon: Just your support.

Rowena: You always have that.

Haldon: What now?

Rowena: I don't know, honey. I'll be down for the holidays. Keep me posted. Ciao.

Haldon: Yeah, later.

Rowena: Hit me up on Facebook. Give me progress report pics.

Haldon: Yeah, I will.

#journeybeginswith5thousand$$

Shī hates Mama because she took all their money. Everything. Took it and gave it to man with busy beard. Breath like cerveza and eyes that always undress her. Mama says Guatemala is no place for indias bonitas. No place for young girls like Shī. Not anymore. Shī asks, what about her, but Mama says, Shī was more important. Go to U.S., Mama says. Go to U.S. and have better life. Coyote tells Mama that all Shī has to do is get across Mexican border, turn self into U.S. Migra and Shī would be free to be American. He also wants 5 thousand dollars, American and a night with Mama. He wanted night with Shi, but Mama won't have it. Threatens to cut off huevos with butcher knife if he tries. Don't know how Mama will protect when Shī is on road with him. Don't know if Mama lets that thought invade. Don't think she wants it to. She cries all night before truck showed up. 4 am. 20 others in back of old truck. Shī doesn't want to leave Mama. Mama is all Shī has left. Papa was killed by gang coming home from mines one night. Al least that is what Mama thinks. That was two weeks ago. Mama struggled to pay for both of them with waitressing and making pan dulce, but not enough. Never enough. Don't know how Mama gets money to pay Coyote. When asked, Mama refuses to tell. Has something to do with man who owns restaurant where Mama works. Shī wants to cry when she got on truck. Mama sees it on her face. But doesn't cry. Mama is always strong. But just before truck pulls away Shī sees single tear fall from corner of Mama's eye glistening in moonlight.

Safety in Numbers

Andrée Greene

"You know, baby," Griffith said as he took a long toke, sitting up so his chest could expand with his inspiration, "numbers… are… holy."

He exhaled grandly, an exclamation point of smoke and mystery, as he passed the joint down to me. I was lying on my back on the floor in front of the couch, listening. Grif stretched out above me, while he explained again why it was necessary to spend twenty-five dollars or more a week on lottery tickets. He went on about various numerical configurations in the Bible and the Koran, Kabbalah, the Tao, how nothing in the universe was random, how there was order in all chaos. This time he segued into the history of the numbers game, explaining how in another era it used to be run in order to help those in need: the widows, abandoned wives and children, the drunks and the down in the mouth; the long in the tooth or bed-ridden and disabled of the neighborhood. But then it got too big for a black man to be making that kind of cheddar, so the mafia muscled in and took over.

I flicked the ash into my hand and dumped it into the big terracotta pot of the rubber tree. Fifteen different plants of various sizes, types, in the living room alone, crowded the huge square glass picture window. In the lamplight, the leaves silhouetted the carpet, my face and body, in a shadow forest. The rubber tree was the largest and its branches arched like a praying mantis over the couch. They were his but I'd always taken care of them as I used to help tend my grandmother's backyard garden.

I'd just started at school again and we could use a little more money, though his twenty-five dollars and climbing ticket money wasn't so much to miss, but what I did miss was the point. It was two in the morning. Grif covered the dinner shifts, late nights, and I'd set the alarm for two or three in the morning depending on the type of restaurant he worked in. He'd arrive either reeking of grease, spices and food, compost of odors, when he got in. He showered and then we'd light candles and talk, listen to music, or have sex, a passionate beat where we'd look each other in the eye, during, after, talk without speaking until I had to get ready for work. Grif read every free moment—always had—-and I was sure what he said was true. He stuck mostly to history or philosophy and religion. He turned me on to the Essenes, the Gospel of Thomas, and esoteric stuff. He was suspicious of my novels, casing my piles of books or removing them from his as if they were counter-intelligence, spies in their midst.

Before I got up and left for bed, he turned on to his back, staring at the ceiling as if it were a campfire sky, "And it won't be like the last time. Hit a few numbers for chump change. It's gonna be the whole thing."

I knew Griffith from when we both lived in the same public housing court. My family's row of two story apartments faced his row in the quad. I could see his kitchen window and back door through the swing set in the middle. I didn't know know him. He was the same age as my older brother and so he didn't speak to twelve year olds. Plus I was bussed up to the heights while he went to the high school downtown. I saw him around mostly by himself, sometimes jogging lightly as if it were just another way of walking a little more quickly. Seldom in a rush, his serene face like an uncut ruby, dark black skin with a glow beneath that reached up into his hair; shiny black sprung springs all over his head gave him an alert yet bewildered air.

We did meet once. The summer before my family moved out. Along with straightening my hair and wearing designer jeans, I wanted to learn to play tennis. Mami refused the iron hot comb, her own afro rivaled the new moon, and I was passing off Kmart brand jeans with the strategic placement of shirt hems to hide the knockoff label. I eventually found her battered wood racket and a can of balls back in the crawl space of the hall storage closet, evidence of my mother's past life before divorce and kids and trying to earn a degree. The top edge was splintered and looked gnawed on from someone dragging it on the ground as they'd walked. I bounced my hand on the racket's flossed face, the top of my head and then my own face, testing the tension. First lightly and then harder, clapping as if it were part of my other hand until the vibration pleasantly twanged up my arms and spread over my body.

I practiced against the brick wall that bookended our apartment row, using the parking lot as my rebound court. Not many people had cars and since we were the first apartment or the last, depending how you looked at it, I could practice volleys while my mother was at work without bothering anyone or smashing windshields. After a week or two of this routine, I heard the faint slam of Griffin's back screen door. From the corner of my eye, I clocked Grif standing at the edge of the lot studying me. I tried to will my pores to dam up or at least to sweat in a more mystifying, less boggy way.

While my back was turned, he appeared at my side, gently gripping my bicep.

"Backhand," Grif said as he sawed my arm back and forth slowly. I stared like a dope at his fingers. He let go and stepped back to watch as I hit some more. The blacktop lot was a hot plancha and still, I could only focus on the warm bracelet, the heat his hands had left on my wrist as he stepped in to show me again. Finally after an energetic bunch of volleys, I whirled around to look for him, only to see his back already across the street,walk-running off to wherever he'd been going before he saw me.

Eight years later, after dropping out of state university, I ran into Griffin in the tiny elevator of the public library. He recognized me as my brother's sister and he looked exactly the same only much taller. He'd been living in Albany, doing nothing special. Now he looked exotic for these parts. He'd grown his hair out on top into large springy ebony coils, shaved low on the sides, half Rasta, half punk that was to me so offhand and natural. Still, when I met my old girlfriends later over fries and pie at the State diner and told them who I'd run into, they considered it queer.

"Well he's f-f-fine all right, was aaaall-ways good looking. But that hair!" Chloe sucked her teeth. "He came back lookin' c-c-crazy—to me anyway," her usual, stuttered "c" stressing the insanity.

"Y'know just doing something a little different doesn't automatically make a guy gay." I rubbed my fingers across my forehead to hide the extent of my irritation.

Chloe rolled her eyes. "Gotta give it to him though. N-n-never c-c-conceited."

Danni added, "Don't even seem to know he cute. Running around town in them tight-ass spandex pants—damn!"

It stunned me again how Chloe talked about Grif as if he were just another guy on the street, another kid from the block. Chloe was Grif's half sister. Although their father, an upright bassist, had married Niecey, Grif's mother, he'd also fathered a checkerboard swath through downtown before taking off to play jazz in Brooklyn. No matter how light-skinned or short the mother was, all his kids were the tallest, wiry and darkest around, including Chloe and her younger brother.

"Puh-leeease," Danni interrupted, "You know full well, he's always been messin with the white girl college students." As she sipped her soda through the left corner of her mouth, she said out the other corner,

"Before AND after he came back. Jordan'd be doing us a public service." Danni said everything out the side of her mouth, with or without straws—out the actual corner, all Mae West-saracastic. "Bring him on back to the fold girl…," slurping her snicker.

I saw him everywhere it seemed after that, including one morning on my way to work. I turned a corner and there he was on one of his jogs, both torch and runner, the mirage in a miracle. He worked in one of the more upscale college-town restaurants where students brought their parents and out-of-towners. I'd hang out at the bar waiting for him to get off and then we'd wander through the night down the gorge steps with the stream garbling along with our talk, leading us downtown. After a few dinners, Thai, Indian, Greek, pizza became our ritual, the walking or riding bikes, the gorges, climbing trails through the woods.

But that's what life always was in this small city. Once you're too old for 4-H or those community center campouts, summers were spent crisscrossing town in packs, Northside to Southside, to what my friends and I called smokeouts or fuckouts. We chased down rumors of Black frat parties we would never be let into up on the hillside campuses, only to drift back down to the Southside, where the small wood frame houses rambled into one another around the project quads. In winter, our steady course interrupted by class buzzers and blizzards. Through an ice-webbed bus or car window, the genuine brilliance of a fresh snowfall, we became as dumbstruck as the waterfalls suspended from the rocks in frozen daggers. At Papa's (because he was the eldest at nineteen of his six siblings), we watched TV and drank beer that he'd buy us, surrounded by soon to be fenced mountain bikes and stereos, much of it stolen from the dorms and apartments of student living. In the warm dusk, dealers and their hangers-on came out on the corners right along with the mosquitoes. Only in cold weather did they huddle alone in the shadow of a telephone pole, empty porches or cornerstones, pacing around the block in forsaken circles with cigarette upon cigarette flashing signals in time with clicking traffic lights on empty frost ashy streets.

"The last time" was six months earlier when Griffith had won $2500. It happened the night I made crespelles, crepes filled with spinach and cheese smothered in an aromatic sauce. My dinners were becoming more elaborate as I grew bored with my receptionist job in a department store office downtown and contemplated school. We lived like students in a first floor apartment in one of the split-up Victorians and worked our service jobs like the townies we were.

Grif supported me all the way.

"If you have the grades you should go," and I could feel his pride in me.

I had made what turned out to be a five-course meal, complete with soup, salad, two entrees—the crespelles and an island pelau—and dessert. I always made meals when he was off, to give him a break from his prep cook job. Turned out his father was Bajan, but Grif knew nothing except music, from the isles. So I often tried to cook something to give him a taste of home.

"I used to love to listen to your mom's talk, yknow her accent when she'd call you guys in and shit."

This time though, I'd started with a soup and couldn't stop, going from one recipe to the next. Grif looked around the table. He seemed to suddenly get a joke and he grinned wide, showing the tiny chip on his front tooth.

"That's a lot of food, babe. "

We both ate, eyeing the dishes as if they were land mines that needed to be dismantled.

All the while, I was getting monthly envelopes from my grandmother with Christian brochures like: AIDS, THE MODERN SCOURGE and $20 or $50 bills tucked in the pages and dodging calls from my mother that always led to the vast mic'd phone silences that magnify and echo all unstated desires and wishes.

He paused mid chew, "I can't taste any garlic. Did you put enough garlic in this?"

"You always say that. I used almost the entire bulb in the sauce."

"Garlic, clean water and ginseng, it's all you need, you'll never get sick."

As I washed the dishes later, I divined the menu for the next day. Fish seemed inevitable. Grif appeared in the doorway. Usually he did the cleanup, order was his delight, but he'd gone into the bedroom after eating with the newspaper. Tomato sauce grease skimmed my arms as I fished the last fork from the sink bottom.

"Look at these for me," he said, stretching his hand out with the ticket and held the winning numbers torn from the newspaper next to it. I craned my neck, back and forth.

"How much do you get with five numbers like that?"

"Twenty-five HUNDRED dollars!" With his eyes clenched, "I almost had it all!"

He dropped to his knees, wrapping his arms around my waist, my thighs, my calves. Still clutching the last fork, I held my dripping hands up like a just scrubbed surgeon as his weight pulled me down.

It was by accident I became involved in Grif's number playing, stumbling on to the gift as Grif put it, on a day I was feeling particularly happy, blessed even. I'd gotten the classes I wanted, and a line on waitress job. I called a used bookstore where I had requested a search on an out of print book by a writer I admired. It had been almost a year.

"Hey-hey, you won't believe this but a copy just came in this morning, big house sale." The bookstore owner was a graying blonde, part of the hippie hangover establishment. His voice was fiending over his new stash, "a mother lode of books, a really sweet haul from an estate sale. I was gonna pull your name out in a few to call you later, just pulling it up. Yup, how about that. You'd be amaaaazed how that happens. Not a lot but sometimes, customers checking the day their book comes in," he drawled on, "It's always so cooool!"

That afternoon when Grif asked me for a number, I thought about that day's date. January 11th and I told him to play the Pick 3 game with 111

"All. The same. Number?" he said in a monotone to emphasize his question. He looked at me as if I'd cursed him out and then softened, "Jordan, those never come out."

He was quiet a minute. "I'll play 1 and 11 in the regular game, so give me five more numbers." As usual whenever he'd ask before, my mind became randomness itself.

Two days later 111 came up in the Pick 3 game. Grif 's gaze was a cocktail of awe and disbelief, "I see…I see…well, swami if you feel that way again, you let me know."

A few days, weeks went by, I didn't look for numbers at first. I told him to play 1259 from a phone number and a digital clock moment that I had.

He played the Pick 4, box. Box meant if they came up in any order he'd win.

"I guess you were wrong," twisting his mouth as he stared at the losing tickets.

Slowly the numbers would rise out of my own daily coincidences and moods and music.

Once, I offered one from the page numbers from books, word count on a paper to the number of birds on a telephone wire, the city bus ticket number. It came up in a different game than the one he played.

"Damn it, Jordan! Can't you tell me *when and how*, which damn game I should play it?"

It went on like that for months. I didn't have a number every week. When I did, he played it and it never won because either he played the numbers on the wrong day or he'd play the wrong game when they came up or the wrong order. The $2500 win was the result of a computer picked number because neither of us had a number. Nevertheless this fact was lost on him.

He pretended to be his usual laid-back self about it all. I could feel him waiting for me, waiting and hoping for a number to reveal itself. That's what he called it, "revealed." Late nights at the library or hanging out after work began to bother him more. I'd invite him along. He'd hesitate, sitting up to consider leaving the apartment with me. Then he'd slump back into place on the couch or walk to another room, shrugging. Or, he pretended that he was too engrossed in a book or cleaning up or whatever to go.

When I did have a number, he'd be happy for days, anticipating the wealth.

"What would you do if you won, anyway?" I asked. "Start that restaurant?"

"If *this* one comes up *this* time, I'll be able to take care of everything, you, me. We could do or go, whatever or wherever we want. Don't you get it? No need for a restaurant."

"Yeah but like what? Buy a house, start a business. Move to the city? Travel?"

He thought for a minute or two, slowly grinning, and speaking slowly, as if enunciation was the problem, "Baby the whole point is you wouldn't have to do anything. You could just be. The end."

As long as there was a numbered chance, his face came to life, his hair stood on its curl in expectation. It always ended the same and I avoided him. His eyes frisked mine when I came home, sure I had a number hidden somewhere. He began to interrogate me about my day to see if he could piece together a number to play. His skin flaked with disappointment when he didn't win or there was no number to play. His hair flagged.

We weren't arguers, too ordinary. And Grif rarely raised his voice and never from anger. Service, curiosity and generosity were our talents. Nevertheless we just snapped over lipstick. I was wearing some to a dean's reception when I never wore any. Why don't I wear it for him, he said, I know you don't like it, I replied.

True enough. How could I explain my attempt to send up a small flare: I am here. Childish. I came home from the reception and cut classes the next day so I could be alone in the apartment since he was working double shift. After turning on the TV, I uncorked one of Grif's bottles of wine he'd brought home from work. He had started studying wines and had quite a stash. I drank it from the bottle while watching talk shows, then an old movie and another bottle and another until I fell asleep on the couch. The next day, I willed a hangover that never really took. Grif's questioning trailed my every move, yet didn't ask anything as I reluctantly unrumpled myself, in the way you smooth like a lost receipt saved from the very top of the trash. That evening I broke up with Grif.

"You're right, you don't have to leave. I will. I have my brother I can stay with until I figure something out." He took only his books, clothes, CDs—classic soul, world reggae, punk— and stereo, left the plants. I was a little ashamed at how much I'd miss the music.

For a month we talked only by phone.

"Maybe we'll get back together," I said, "when you figure out what you want to do, to be. You're too unhappy," I said.

"I dunno, I get that you're looking out for me in a way. I do get it." He sighed, "I'm not un-happy though Jor. Not how you think I am anyway."

When I got lonely, I'd sit with the plants, trace patterns in the dirt, dust their leaves. Once we met for lunch and his eyes looked murky and red although he tried to play it off and be upbeat. I returned to the apartment we'd shared. I was about to ditch the place. I couldn't afford it on my own. In the refrigerator I had saved the gross white crème center of a couple packs of Oreos, scraped them into plastic sandwich bag as Danni and I heckled a weekend marathon of movie videos. I drew a square on the wall and shaped the chilled Oreo icing into a good-sized ball, chilled it again, and then lobbed the Oreo ball around thirty times from across the room into the square successfully before the icing's shape yielded.

Another month and I sat at one end of the couch as Chris, a short engineer grad student from Chicago, sat at the other. Nervous, I picked at the label that had softened on the moist bottle. Peeling off the bar code, the numbers typed beneath the black and white thick-thin stripes, its order gradually took form: month day year. It was my birthday.

"Hey look it's my birthday on the barcode." I said aloud before I could think. Something soft and pulpy as the edges of a label sank in my chest as soon it slipped out. I noted the brand of the beer to distract myself.

"Really? Kinda cool, yeah?" He paused, frowned "Ooo and a little weird too," and he did Twilight Zone music, wiggling his fingers in my face, flicking water drops from the bottle's condensation and started to try to tickle me.

As I pushed a smile, how could it feel so planned when it wasn't? I could see it all unfold before it actually did, the tickling and then the kissing, my eyes widen and his pores, and tight sideburns the heavy foreign topography of his square body beneath his clothes. Then hearing the front door inhale as it swung open just as I remembered at that exact moment that I hadn't locked it. And there was Grif. Eyes lit and sweating a sweet boozy liquor.

"How c-co-ooould you," in a smothered wail, its accusation still plain. He didn't move again. He stood where he was as if awaiting a fate both under his feet and beneath him. Chris walked carefully around him as he did the male ram settle-down dance to Grif's shaky yet simmering chest bump. I had told Chris to leave as I kept reassuring that I'd be fine and followed him to the door. Griffith would never hurt me, anyone. Plus, I thought to myself, fair's fair. Hadn't I disturbed his peace?

"That's right leave!" Grif shouted from the living room, murmuring loudly "she don't know *what* she's doin'. What IS she do-ing…here? here? here? here? Where'd she go?"

When I got back, Grif had pulled every plant out of its pot, including the rubber tree, which languished across the couch, a diva now suffering from the vapors. The rest were jumbled nebulas of stalks, and lolling leaves, their exposed roots and broken stems in clumps of speckled starry soil that dusted all over the coffee table, floor and chairs. I looked around, avoiding his eyes, tangling my fingers in sympathy with the scene before me. I knelt down to place in its half-filled pot, the plant closest to me, a variegated jade tree that never could get enough sun lately, dropping its thick leaves, often at the slightest touch.

Grif stared down at me for a long while and the evening's natural light made our silence and its troubled current sparkle. No, I wasn't scared of Grif, only of what couldn't be asked and answered, or really ever understood beyond a rattle or hiss in the heart.

At last, he took a step forward and slapped the plant and pot out of my hands. And then, he left.

The following day, I turned the channel to the numbered ball drawing at 7:30. And again the next day, and the next one after that. No ticket, just wanted to see if those last digits would play out. But then I stopped. I knew my date would not come up until I quit watching out for it.

Interrogation

Cathy Guo

He is perfect to whom the entire world is as a foreign place –Saint Victor

Evening wanderings past the trickle
mark at the beginning of the Yellow River
a handful of sand lilies scooped from its bank
peeled then boiled, the petals on your tongue
a dissolvable yearning for aftertaste
(the pedal which asks the song to linger):
we have parched needs in parched lands.

The river refills the wine-cup
the absence in one hand cancels itself
and the hand plucks out a sound—
muted *erhu* from the courtyard below
where the old folk are dancing
earthbound to Maoist tunes.

I awaken each morning to think
that I am hearing it again, and the
question—is this still exile
or has the entire world finally become
that sweet and foreign place?

My Great Grandmother in the Kitchen

Alexandria Delcourt

She watches me, her transparent face reflecting in panes of glass, echoing in gas stove smoke. Her laugh: shifting stacks of drying dishes, a whisper of black hair falling over my neck. I feel her next to me as if one hundred years could fit inside this kitchen, as if the floor were tiled with winter after winter and I could walk across them into the empty corners where she once stood. I see the red curve of her hips in the mirror, dream her blue butterfly's dress swirling in the dust of midnight phonograph.

I only have stories of her feet pounding on naked earth, of her blinded children running through a jungle humid with bullets—this history draws these words from hidden shades of red caged within my breathing body. Blood is an almost-miracle that way, how it stretches across centuries, oceans even, to fill the empty seats at our tables, reverses the forward passing of time, chasm of memory, to stare back at us from inside cracking mirrors, to help us take that first step. Then the second. Then the third.

poet: rigor mortis, zombies, & dehumanization

Raina J. León

after Night of the Living Dead *(1968), 1:34:35, directed by George A. Romero and in response to the rise of zombie films*

it ends with a bullet to the head
or a sickle machete spiked bat
any dead-em will do

livor mortis rigor mortis algor mortis
body cools blood stains the skin fixed in its timelessness
days it takes to blacken
first the extending green divines rotting flesh
some gods blue & some gods kelp
purple bruise & then black
that's real

only movies go bite + time = skin slip & black blood spurt

in truth
eyes protrude & challenge tongue
intestines reveal their tangle
push through vagina & rectum

black people have no futures
in sci-fi or horror

white man apocalypse :
whiteness grays & turns black
dark skin lost earth crow black eyes or embalmed roll-white

we always die first in the movies
when death leads to
black behind boards

how dare those zombies crave
beasts
everyone needs a cure

it all ends with a bullet
& a bonfire
zombies aren't human

drag that out of here

i keep searching my head for holes
practicing, *stop. don't shoot. i'm alive.*

Swimming Lesson

Kelsey Valadez

I found a pool and fell in. The water surrounds me while the light reflects and refracts; this is harmonious distortion. Underwater, I'm learning how to swim. I have learned to love the water; swimming is no longer a chore. I am swimming past the memories that consumed me like the water, and the places where we slept.

The gods are not dead, but sleeping. The gods are not dead, but forgotten. The gods are breathing; I feel the life in the wind blowing through my window. And then, when I think of holding you here, I can't think of a more intimate act than awakening the gods with my love.

When we sleep, there are no sirens, only gods. And when we sleep, your hands are two distinct halves of the only pair I want touching me.

You and I are two halves looking for each other in the dark, underwater.

A Talent for Packing

Leticia Hernández-Linares

We grab the bags, half filled,
again. Let the shame we own
shade us as we run.

In the night, women whisper
about the diameter of the bruises
and extent of their captivity.

Do you remember, can you imagine.

The phone rings, the boy sounds rescue calls
into my ears. His hands throwing this terrible
back at me. How do you comb trauma
into his hair? How do you refuse it?

We pack bags furiously, with flawless precision.
Essentials, everything else can be acquired.
She jokes that we resemble gitanos. We
don't laugh, respectfully understand,

we don't have a home; bags spill
out our foundation, Nina singing

'Either Way I Lose,' in my head, as I throw
away my chance to pretend regular.

Silly refrain in the background—why
can't we clank tea cups, laugh softly?
Our silhouettes
are cut from metal
and we don't drink tea.

Medea to Susan Smith, 1995

Erin Koehler

It would have been better if we both had guns/if it had been over more quickly maybe we would have had more time to grieve, to feel a guilt bigger than fire & lake. There's always the hypothetical: what if your family wasn't an ache full of cemeteries, or the hushed clink of your second father's belt buckle. What if you weren't father haunted—& what if they believed you. But those things did happen & that leads us to our camaraderie: terrors where stairs are collapsing & the traffic lights hunt somebody. I've been meaning to ask you, when it was over, how did you re-learn to fill glasses of water/windows of water? While on the subject: that thing about the hand on the window—do you pretend you imagined it? I know the feeling. I can't use the teakettle anymore/the whistle-scream ache into flashback. I shudder away with the visions: I'm suspended in cobwebs, strings plucked & bound by my ankles/my wrists, hear the clicking of pincers, but never quite see them. Is that what it's like where you are? I forget you don't have a chariot to take you into sun—lungs still pink, still forced to remember: betrayals ripen to perfection, then spoil.

Upon Viewing my Daughter Drowning as a [Continuous Loop]

Erin Koehler

the water is deafness
pulling a string
of silence out of my
ears / when she slips
under the surface each
time I am frozen &
moving /she dips/ the
water grabs her /this
deafness slicing me
dragging me naked
my body granulates
disintegrates & bends
/ her eyes have
changed they have lost
sunlight / mine lost
to these anxieties
of motherhood how
tomovequickenough /
I can not dive cannot
/repeat/ cannot unsee
the fingertips pressing
her eyes closed / water
pulls salt from her
mouth & [jump]

Almost Animal

Didi Jackson

I heard they no longer sew eyelids of the dead shut.

When I pressed my palm to his wrapped chest
it was an abbreviation for marriage.

And as I left the morgue that day,
I emptied the room—I carried him on my back
and over my shoulders. I carried him
across my forehead and between my shins.

At home, I molded a ball and cannon.
This was my way of waging war on suicide.
I didn't eat, and I slept only some of the nights.

Do you think I chipped away at the day
the same way I did the night?

There was nothing left for me to look at
so I closed my own eyes.
I wore sunglasses and a light jacket.
I wore them until I met my future husband.

Until then, I busied myself counting the lacerations
on my dead husband's neck and wrists.
I am good with numbers.

I didn't spend all this time counting
just to get so far in front of him.
But the hours I waited for him
layered like moths around a weak light.
I wanted to burn the holding room and sell its ashes.

After the dried blood was wiped from his face,
his jaw was set with a piece of string.
They tried to leave a natural appearance.

His throat was a village; my palm an iron of matrimony.
I wanted to smooth his clothes; I wanted to clean his hair.
I should have been the one to prepare his body.

It would have been easier that way.
But it didn't matter,
he was going right into the fire.

Rio Bravo

Robin Scofield

I. Pass to the South

In Texas, we say The Valley as though there is no
other, yet from the red rock ridge twisted with creosote
in El Paso, I can see another full of corn, tomate,
y lechuga, far from where the Rio Grande cuts
canyons, farther from those orange orchards
whose sweetness is capitalized in spring.
Now upriver
many years between the Upper Valley
and North Peak, I cannot chip words
from shells in caliche that hint at the past,
the cretaceous sea that won't give up
its secret name which is not the sound
of fountains nor cathedral bells.

II. Mexico's Central Highlands

Nor is it El Cordero de Dios, the taste of God.
The feast is for hungry ghosts who want

to taste the lamb before it takes a breath
and sullies its flesh.
But you can't get lamb around San Miguel
because the food is local, alive in the field
this morning. Yesterday, I saw a man carry
a cow leg to the market on his shoulder.
At Bellas Artes, we have to be satisfied
with the sound of water. Leaves rot,
the lamb's nose is chipped. Bitter oranges
thrive next to thick adobe walls that keep
the cold and damp in. I taste the season,
la rosca with nuts and fruit
and a plastic white baby, so I bite gingerly
while Carl who's Jewish gets it every year.

III. A Knot of Hawks

Hawks weigh in,
featherlight in the thermal flow rising
from the canyon floor. We have to fight
through the market not to commit idolatry
three times a day at the loading dock
where the holy family kneels by the Christ child.
The wind pushes me back in my mind
as I look up from the Texas Mountain Laurel
into the yellow eye of a snow-breasted hawk.
The electric pole gives him a street view of doves.
I am home, and here is the name come to perch, to hunt,
as my son opens a compass and gives it to me.
For when you get lost, he says.

IV. Pass to the North

When I am south at eye level with the hawk
on the hill with three crosses, I keep my
compass in my hand. I go up the gully
Calle de la Luz, limestone dust,
cross over a muddy stream with cloven
hoofprints, meet the goats who don't want
to meet me. I see what an easy seat the boy
has on his mare, how the western sun
bronzes them into one being.

Calling Collect from Prison / Father-Daughter Intermediary

Amy Elizabeth Bishop

:::: Tell her
    Tuesdays are good days   —I know
    making time is hard. Make sure she is reading
        —make sure she stays
in school; tell her
                keep your nails ragged as an architect's
               first skyline to serrate
    bodies that want
to claim   you, as if claiming is all
        they know   how to do.
Teach her to throw   a punch:
    remember to leave
  your thumb exposed—she'll learn
        after the first time she breaks
                        a knuckle.
                            ::::   Tell her:
how we buried baby teeth/first
    haircut/christening clothes in a prayer
chest. How precious   how adored   how
many hours on our knees—
        Tell her   —send
 a school picture to show

—to fall asleep with—
        smile like waking   to birthday/Christmas mornings.
Tell her I would turn
    this world color-blind
      for her :::: don't tell her how much I miss
   her/don't tell I called/don't tell

The choices we make

Araceli Esparza

She said to me the word is sacred;
in the beginning, there was el verbo.
My heart is pinned not by needles but by type-faced letters,
purple rock crystals I've seen you before as a child.
I think she was with me.

Was it in Mexico they gave us a sheet of small crystals glued on?
But exactly where? Guanajuato?
San Juan de Los Lagos? Irapuato?
Dirt roads, stony crumbling sidewalks,
Dusty broken corners, laughing eyes, knowing I didn't belong,
I moved back behind Abuelita.

Porque me estan viendo—I peep.
Someone says, ojo
Abuelita says, no creemos en eso
They are looking at me—I counter.
No los veas, she remedies.
Pero. I'm looking for small
pieces of my face in their faces.
Isn't this where I belong?
Her hair—I want hair like that.

His eyes—Wish they could be mine.
Those hands—I've seen before.

I stepped all where I have stepped.
At the bottom, there was a freshly covered
snowland, perfectly unconquered.
Until I stepped.

You Can Always Tell

H. N. Holder

Afterwards, I stayed in the position that Sunil had left me before he went to the bathroom. I was trying to read my body like it was a handful of bones thrown on the sheet. It was missionary that time, legs spread, arms on either side of my head with the elbows bent, palms open. Sunil had put my panty, a white lacy thing, across my stomach so it wouldn't make that sound he hated. My belly has two folds of fat, one just under my bobbies, and another under my navel. The flat place between the fat sweats when we're doing it, and it makes this noise, like trying to pull your foot out of thick mud. A song came from between my legs. Hmmm. If anything was slightly off it was the bobbies. I touched one and looked at the brown swelling with its large nipple like a raisin hat. Sunil barely touched them throughout the whole business. Weird. Last year, on his last night in Trinidad, I had to beg him to stop trying to suck my heart through them. He looked up at me, laughed then his pale cheeks turned red and before I knew it, he was crying and talking with webs of saliva across the cave of his mouth, "I don't want to go, Resh. Tell your father to cash the ticket and I could stay. Me and you… blah, blah, blah… could get married… have a good life in Trinidad…." He had no land, no business, nothing and wanted to get married to woman like me. Daddy was sending him to school and planned to give him some businesses to run when he returned to Trini. That way poor Sunil from Princes Town would have more than looks and fair skin when we get married.

The water stopped falling in the shower and I looked up at the ceiling and at the walls. A single, uncovered light bulb was at the center of a stucco ceiling above the bed. Glossy white paint showed every pit and dried paint drip on the walls. Effing ugly.

"What you thinking about?" His voice was the same. Deep. I felt it in my chest. He held the towel around his waist with one hand. I closed my legs and turned to face him. The roses he had given me at the airport the night before were in a vase on the nightstand. They smelled sour and the edges of the petals were black.

"About the fock."

"What?" He laughed and the gray eyes that caught my attention in secondary school ten years ago sparkled, like a cream soda in a glass in the sun. He got handsomer since he went away.

"You hiding from me, Sunil?" I pointed at the towel. "I done see everything so—"

"Resh, you start to give trouble already?" He smiled, retied the towel around his chest, held the knot with one hand and pursed his lips.

I sat up. "Let the towel go."

He sucked his teeth, the sound like paper tearing.

"I want to see it. The thing Daddy send away."

He let the towel go.

"Turn around."

He turned his ass to me.

"No, not so…" I laughed "I want to see it from the side, to see if it hanging right."

"Resh, you ain't change, oui. Still crazy." He turned and put both palms behind his head. I watched every crease. Every hair. I was wondering how he thought the sex was. But if I asked him, he might know that I cared about what he thought. Not my scene to come off like that.

"You finish?" He gyrated his hips then thrust them forward, everything swinging.

"Sunil, stop! I still looking...Ok, Ok, I done. The hair too long. Trim it like you used to have it."

He nodded and walked around the bed to the chest of draws to get dressed.

"You going to trim it right?"

"Resh, I leaving my balls just so. I can't even tell you how to cut your hair." He zipped his pants up. "You not getting up to bathe?"

I was kinda annoyed about the balls comment, but couldn't stop looking at the walls. It was like each dent was pulling me in.

"You don't like the place?" he asked.

"No, is not...I know you don't like to talk about money, Sunil, but... if you needed more money to live on, you could've told me, and I or Daddy could've —"

"Resh, you and your father paying for school...giving me a allowance every month. I comfortable here."

"Is just that I thought...I thought it would've been nicer. We talk on the phone all the time and you never say it was like this. The area nice? At least?"

"This is Brooklyn. East Flatbush. Is a nice area." A line formed on his perfect forehead. "But it always have something nicer. And this place might look bad compared to ...what you accustomed to, but the rent here is high, even for Brooklyn. Plus the woman who own the house, Mrs. Mannix...she from Antigua, she don't bother me. You should hear the horror stories other people who come to this country have. Coming home and finding the landlord in your place, people making noise so you can't study..."

While he talked, he folded his arms and, with one hand, played with his chest hairs. I looked at the fingers pulling the thick dark hairs then back to his mouth, like Shahid Kapoor's mouth.

"….not fixing anything. And Caribbean people are the worst landlords. They just don't get the tenant thing. They think anybody living in their house is a child even if they paying rent." He stopped, took a t-shirt from the draw and put it on. "You don't know, Resh. You don't know."

"I forget how you could go on and on when you want to make a point. I get it. You comfortable here and you don't want we money." I was effing vex. The idea that he would bring me to a place like this then try to justify it by making it about money. Like he ever had to think about money since we been together. I wrapped the sheet around me and got up.

"Now you hiding from me," Sunil said.

I didn't answer.

"You vex, Resh? Don't be vex. You just reach. You want to stay in the hotel instead? I could stay there with you 'till you leave."

"No, I go stay." I went to the bathroom.

The next day, a Thursday, after Sunil went to class, I tried to watch TV on my laptop but Daddy and my sister, Sharma, kept texting me. Sharma and me manage two stores and a nightclub, Club Space. Every text was about deliveries, workers and the band for Saturday. I texted Daddy to say that I was all right, and told Sharma to do whatever. I was on vacation for eff sake.

In the bedroom, Sunil had made the bed. The roses were bent over, trying to kiss the nightstand with their stale, red lips. I lifted the mattress. An old t-shirt and a pair of jeans lay on top of four wide planks of plywood that ran across a metal frame. There were clothes in all the draws. Not a lot. I checked the tags. Regular brands. And two pairs of shoes under the bed, some brown leather dressy business and sneakers. That's three pairs, counting the one he was wearing. A few things in the closet. No coats. I showered, got dressed and went out.

Outside was so bright that I had to cover my eyes from the white light bouncing off the chrome of cars parked across the street. I walked up the narrow, bare concrete steps that led from Sunil's basement apartment to the yard. Spring was teasing the yard and a few light blue flowers littered the short grass. I went up some red painted steps to the front door of the house. I didn't notice the night before, but it was a gray brownstone. The door was varnished wood with clear glass panels. Just inside the door, I saw some flip-flops and a woman's worn, black strappy sandals. I pressed the white doorbell that jutted from the wall like a pimple. Nothing. Again. I heard footsteps coming toward the door.

Mrs. Mannix opened the inner door, varnished wood too, and looked out. She narrowed her small dark eyes and leaned her head to one side so I waved and pointed toward the basement. She mouthed, Oh, and opened the door.

"Hello, I'm Sunil girlfriend. Reshma Boodoo." I shook her hand.

"Yes. He tell me you was coming, see." Her accent sounded strange. She was fair skinned. Black and Chinese mix probably. Her gray hair was in plaits like a girl.

"I just…wanted to say hello. In case you see me in the yard and was wondering who I was."

"Ok. You had a good flight comin' in?"

"Yes. Smooth. I landed right?" I laughed because I didn't know what else to do. "So, Sunil ask me to pay the rent. He didn't have any time this morning." I took out the money. "How much, again?"

"Rent not due till next week. He payin' early?" I saw her round shoulders move back under the shiny, yellow polyester.

"Yes. We might'nt be here next week. How much again? He forget to separate the rent money from the bills money."

"Seven."

I counted it out.

"Wait for a receipt." She turned and went inside.

As I walked out of Troy Avenue onto Church Avenue, I heard the receipt crinkling in the pocket of my leather jacket and shoved it in deeper. It was just before midday, so there were few people on the street. I had been to New York many times, but never to a poor people place like this. I passed stores with racks of clothes outside that said, '2 for $5.' There seemed to be a vegetable market on every corner with rows of oranges, pears, apples and other goods inside and outside. I watched a man cut the blackened, spongy ends from some carrots with a short cutlass, wrap it in plastic and Styrofoam and put it on a table with other fruits and vegetables that said, '50c Any one.' In between the cheap clothes, vege-marts and beauty-stores were churches. Church of Christ. Eglise Baptiste Haitienne. They opened right on the pavement, some of them next to restaurants with only a gate to, I suppose, separate the sheep from the goats. The fanciest shoulder-high gate was in front one New Community Church. A short dark skinned man in a shining, technicolor outfit, like country come to town, was behind it. He told me good morning and asked me if God was good. And all I could think of was the receipt in my pocket and how I was searching Sunil's place. I held my head up and walked to the train station at Nostrand Avenue. The little technicolor man started singing some hymn. The sound stayed in my head long after I could actually hear him. Even the rumbling of the subway train couldn't drown it out.

Later that day, I heard the key slide in the lock and stood up. Then sat down and pretended to stare at the laptop. I let Sunil call me twice before I answered. "Yeah." You must never be eager.

"Hon, you stay inside whole day?" He was at the living room door. When I didn't turn around, he walked over and kissed me on the cheek. He smelled like cologne plus clothes plus a slight sweaty, man smell.

The lower fold of my belly pitched forward a little. Ok, a lot.

"You went out?" He put down his knapsack.

I turned around and shrugged. "No, I wear makeup to stay home."

He smiled. "You eat something? Want me to buy some food?"

"Yeah. I kinda hungry. But…"

"But?"

"I got some things for you today."

"O Lord, Resh." He said it like he was fed-up or something.

My face was probably looking vexed, because he changed his tune. "What you got?"

I ran passed him to the bedroom and pointed to the bags on the floor.

"Saks?" He sighed loudly.

"I see you don't have any good clothes. And you need sheets for this bed. Plus I want to go out. Party."

He sat on the bed and I reached for the first bag. "I want to go this Saturday. And I want to see where you go to school, Brock College."

"Baruch College. Bah-rook." He lifted his small womanish chin.

"Look at you nah? Telling me how to pronounce. Fine, I want to see Baruch College and when we finish trying on clothes, I want something to eat. Nothing from around here." I wrinkled my face. "From online."

He seemed frozen, looking at me and at the same time looking passed me to the bathroom door.

"Sunil, you hear me?"

"Yes. Try on. Food. Party Saturday. Show she Bah-rook."

"Ok. Try this one on first." I picked up a bag and took out a blazer.

He was staring passed me again.

"Sunil?"

"Reshma?" he mocked.

On Saturday, my father called. He wanted to make sure I wasn't staying with Sunil. Imagine, in this day and age Daddy trying to convince himself that his daughters are pure. Geez.

"No, Daddy. I at the hotel and Sunil coming to pick me up." I put one finger across my lips when Sunil came out the bathroom and pointed at the phone. Then Daddy was going on about the store in San Fernando and blah, blah, blah. Then his voice got school teacherish, "Reshma, how things going with Sunil?"

"How you mean?" I changed the tone of my voice to match his.

"He alright? He going to school?"

I walked to the farthest corner of the living room. "He in school. Going to see the school next week."

"Ok, that is all I want to know. Because people tell me not to do this thing. Not to send a next man son to school and give him business to run. The pundit and all say is not a good thing. That I lucky with girl children and not boy children. And is not…"

Sunil came into the room and spun around. He was in the Zegna pale pinkish, taupish, don't know how to describe it, cotton pants, with the navy Zegna blazer and white shirt. Some pale Calvin sneakers to bring it down a notch.

"…because you want it—" Daddy was still talking.

"Daddy, Sunil reach. I have to go."

"Let me talk to him, nah?"

"Next time, we runnin' late. Call tomorrow." I touched the red bar across the screen.

I screamed. He was looking so effing hot.

"Shhh…Resh. Mrs. Mannix." He put his palms up, and widened his eyes. That night they were cream soda with flecks of gold.

I went to the mirror on the closet door to check myself. The girdle panty made my stomach look flat in the red Bebe mini sheath dress. My face looked like a brown Lakshmi murti, heavy black lined eyes and thin red lips. Black C L heels made good legs look model great, with long thick, dark hair to my behind. Just that alone was half of what all Indian men wanted. The other half was to know how to make sada roti from scratch. Bilnah. Ghee and Tawah. Flip it hot with one oily hand, and watch it swell like a young girl's belly, the whole nine. But my mother died when I was in primary school so I never learned to cook. So Sunil was only getting half of a good Indian woman. Daddy never brought another woman in the house. So Sharma and me grew up on KFC and buy-food. I know Daddy has a woman. Sometimes, on the phone, I hear a woman's voice in the background. Other times Chris, our Negro driver, is out all day. I'm home, Daddy is home, Sharma is in the store. So who is the chauffeur chauffeuring then? When I pile in the car to go out on those evenings, the backseat smells like perfume.

That night, we went to Giocare, Aniello's club, on 50th and 9th Avenue. Aniello has a face like a Greek statue from a museum with a short compact, chiseled body to match. I met him when he came to my nightclub, Club Space, in Trinidad last year and had promised to visit his club when I was in New York. So we got the royal treatment. We were in the back in a private leather booth with Aniello's friends and his wife, Shari, a tall, gorgeous Negro woman from Martinique with big wild hair and a vacant look in her brown eyes. The friends? Ehhh. Club flies I call them, because every popular club has them flitting around until they find a hotter place to go to. Oldish well-dressed businessmen types with some pretty, pretty, thin, thin girl on their arm that they were trying to impress. There was a glass paneled private bar with small cask whiskey, champagne, everything. Men in tight, black clothes and aprons kept bringing out platters of food with shrimp and two-color caviar, and every kind of dessert you could think of. Our table had a clear crystal bowl of coke. I snorted two fingertips worth, enough to sharpen the edges and brighten the colors. Aniello had some white pills, like coated aspirin, in his pocket. He took two after I refused him, one for me and one for him, he said.

All night, Aniello kept trying to pour Sunil's drinks. After the pills kicked in, he got brave and ran his hands along Sunil's thighs and commented on how soft the cotton on his pants was. But he had a thick Italian accent and soft sounded like suck. "Tha fabreek ez soooo suck." So Sunil crossed his legs and spent most of the night away from the private booth in a chair against the wall with his face pinched, his eyes in shadow. He was too angry to notice that some of the thin, pretty girls and Shari had their doll's eyes on him too. I danced all night with Aniello, with Shari, with the club flies, with everybody. The whole time, I felt Sunil's eyes on me, gray laser beams that burned my legs and cut holes in my dress, like that fella from X-men. The good-looking one with the shades, who was toting it for Jean Gray. But I never looked at Sunil once. Around 3 am, the DJ played a soca and reggae mix for us and just so, Sunil was up and dancing. He was behind me wining, one arm across my chest, just under my bobbies, at the top of the girdle. I bent over and gyrated on the crotch of his suck cotton pants. My hair stuck to me, like warm, wet palms holding both cheeks. Through the corner of one eye, in the mirror near the bar, I saw us. Some tall, well-dressed man was peeing a big splotch of red paint. And I laughed, loud and crazy, like an argument just under the sound of the music. I was still giggling to myself when we got in the taxi at daybreak to go home.

He was kissing my stomach, and I blurted it out. "Where your coats? They not in the closet."

"Hmmm." He kissed my navel. "By the laundromat."

"And your clothes? You hardly have any clothes here. And how many coats you have?" The sensation of the last kiss lingered and I pushed it from my mind and lifted my head so that I could look at him.

"Now, Resh?"

"Yeah."

He supported himself on his arms. His head and chest swung like a hammock, casting a shadow over my middle. The valley between the folds got dark. "I don't have much clothes cause I don't need much. My coats are in the Golden Touch Laundromat on 45th and Church Avenue." He pronounced each word like he was a reading the news. "I have two coats. A dark blue pea coat and a green down jacket. Since it is May, my leather jacket is warm enough. This is Dominic Kalipersad reporting for TV Six News."

I tried to study his face.

"Sooo, we could fock now?"

I let my head drop to the bed.

He kissed my folds and worked his way down to where the hairs began. Just when I thought he was going to come back to my lips, I felt something warm and wet between my legs. I waited to see what I would feel. Something moist, like being touched with sticky hands.

"Sunil, What you doing?"

He looked up at me and pulled his tongue in. "I thought you like that?"

"No, Sunil! I never like that."

"Resh is…"

"I like to fock, Sunil! Dick! And throwing waist. That is me. That lickin' business is… Some girl like you to lick she, but that girl is not Reshma. Who like you to lick she?"

"How you mean?" He was supporting himself on his arms again.

"Who like you to lick she when you fock she?"

"Resh. Nobody. Is just that I wanted…to taste you. So when you go, I could remember you. Never forget you." His face was red and his eyes had a wet sheen to them, like he was about to cry. It was like his last night in Trinidad again and I felt like a wicked woman. So I sat up, held his face in my hands and kissed him on the mouth. "Sorry, Honey.

Sorry. Is just that," I kissed one cheek. "You here and I there and," I kissed the other cheek, "I hear all these stories about people going away and being with other people." I kissed his mouth again. "Sorry, Sorry. Is just that the lickin' thing is not my scene. You know?"

He was still for a moment then he kissed my mouth and went back to my stomach. When he got to the end of that stretch of land, he worked his way up to my bobbies and neck. Once he was inside, I closed my eyes and moved fast, trying to rub away the wet sticky feeling he had put between my legs. When I was near the top of my mountain, I opened my eyes and looked up at Sunil. His eyes were like slits and there was a line in his brow, like he was trying to see something clearly. But the image wouldn't stay in my head because my head was touching the sky.

At Baruch College, we sat together at the back of a large lecture hall that slanted downwards. A tall white-haired professor lectured at the front with a red laser pointer and PowerPoint slides. Most of the people in the Intro to Finance class were Chinese and Indians. There were a couple White people and some Negro people, mostly Africans Sunil said, who attended classes in three-piece suits. Sunil introduced me to some of his friends. There was Amadou, an African guy from somewhere I don't remember and the rest were Indians and Negroes from Trinidad. There was another Sunil, dark, fat and hairy, not like my Sunil, his girlfriend, Nadine, a fair-skinned Indian girl who was in a hoodie and jeans with her hair piled at the top of her head, with no makeup whatsoever. And two Negro fellas, Jason and Nigel. Nigel said he was from San Fernando and that he knew me, but I didn't know him. After class, we went to a dumpling place nearby.

The dumpling place, Pot Stickers, was a long red counter with stools against a glass wall that looked out to the street, with some black chairs and small red tables at the back. We had ordered online during the lecture, picked up and sat at one of the tables. Hairy Sunil and Nadine came with us, but took their food and left. After, Sunil was telling me how Hairy Sunil and Nadine lived together in some apartment near Baruch and wanted to open a business together. Then he started talking about how Amadou wanted to become the president of his country and that Nigel and Jason were planning to return to Trinidad to get into politics.

"Anyhow," I said, "How come you don't have any Indian friends?" I had my back to the door and turned around because I heard laughter and loud talking. A group of Chinese looking girls came in, all pretty faces and long, straight dark hair.

"And Sunil and Nadine are?" He stuck a fork in a dumpling and put it in his mouth.

"I mean like Indian Indian. From India. So many of them in this school and you don't have one Indian friend?"

He leaned forward. "Resh, Indians from India don't want to be friends with people like me. And they not just from India, they from all over. Bangladesh, Pakistan, Sri-Lanka, Africa and all. Most of them talk Urdu, Gujrati, languages I never hear about. As soon as they realize I don't speak the language, they cut me off." He swiped a hand near his neck like he was cutting it off. "Plus, to them, we went to Trinidad as indentured laborers, slaves really. We from the lowest class, or caste or whatever, in their eyes. They don't want to have anything to do with—"

"Indian is Indian, Sunil."

"Yeah, Trini-Indians like to think that." He shrugged his shoulders, leaned back in his chair and dropped his plastic fork.

"Anyway, you sure you approaching these Indians, Pakistanis, or whatever in the right way?"

"Like I say, I might look like them, but we not the same. I tell one of them that my mother name Drupatee and he started laughing. He said no one in India would ever name their daughter that. You know how many Trini and Guyanese Indian girls go out with Indian fellas, in a serious relationship, thinking they going to get married, only to wake up one morning to find he unfriend them on Facebook and block their number because he in India getting married to a real Indian. Who his parents pick."

The noisy group was in front of me. They were dragging chairs and tables so they could sit together. I had to raise my voice over the dull sound of wood scraping tile. "Sunil, I have friends. From India. Who come to Trinidad to visit me." I leaned back in my chair too.

"So! You have money. They have money. That is what you have in common. And you are Steven Boodoo daughter." He sounded vexed. "Don't act you don't know that that has something to do with it…" He looked at something behind me.

"Sunny!" A voice behind me said.

"Hey," Sunil said when she stood next to our table.

"Padma. My girlfriend, Reshma. Visiting from Trinidad. Reshma. Padma." He pointed at both of us. She put out her hand to shake mine and I took it. "Nice to meet you," I said.

"Same here. Sunny talk about you all the time." She was my complexion, with smooth skin like an airbrushed picture, and she wasn't wearing anything but lipstick. Thick dark hair that had waves like a stale roller set. And the shape? Coke in the bottle, flat belly, small waist, hips and big, big bobbies. A cleavage, like four inches long, was showing at the front of her white t-shirt with the denim jacket over it.

"I ordered during class and just came to pick up, so—" she began.

"You could eat with us if you want." Sunil looked at me for confirmation.

"Yeah, bring your food."

"Ok." She turned to go to the counter. Big round ass in her skinny jeans.

She sat with us and talked while she ate her chicken dumplings. She was from Princes Town just like Sunil. Only people from P-town call him Sunny. (I was wondering about that too, at first.) Said she went to San Fernando Secondary one year behind me. That would make her 23, a year younger than Sunil and me. But she looked 18 or 19. Anyway, I didn't remember her. She could have been any one of the groups of girls, a blur of pleated, brown skirts and white sneakers, who walked to the taxi-stand, rain or shine, while our driver picked us up, and Sharma and me argued over whose turn it was to choose a CD to play on the way to lessons.

She was in the same accounting class as Sunil, and came to Pot-Stickers after her English class every Wednesday. She mentioned Amadou and Nadine a few times so I guess she was part of the group. I didn't talk on purpose because I wanted her to feel like a third wheel and leave. But Sunil kept asking her questions and looking at me while she spoke, like I was the one who wanted to know the answers. When I couldn't take it anymore, "So, you planning to go home when you finish with your degree?" I asked.

She laughed and her bosom shook, like it was soft and light. "No. I want to stay. It don't have nothing home for me. Where I will get a job? I don't want to work for the public service. My parents don't have connections. Plus I have smaller brothers and sister I have to help my parents mind."

"Sunil going back, you know." I hoped my eyes sparkled.

"Yeah. He tell me." She looked at him, put the dirty napkins in the empty dumpling box, and held the box with both hands. "He have business and everything waiting for him when he go back. Sunny just lucky."

"Yes, he is. My lucky man." Sunil had his elbows on the table. I reached across and held one, hoping that he would extend his arm and hold mine. He didn't so I held on to the fabric of his jacket, and rubbed the elbow underneath with one finger.

"You going to college too?" She asked.

"Me?" I laughed. "I have life experience. I running business. Business-es. Since I leave high school. I don't need a business degree." That was a blow she was trying to throw at me. Imagine. "Not like people like you, who don't have business in their blood and have to go to school to learn about it."

She moved the box closer to her and moved back in her chair.

I held on to Sunil's other elbow and he stretched out his hands so that they lay on mine. She got up. "Well. Nice to meet you, Reshma. Sunil. See you in class next week, if not before." She smiled, turned and I watched Sunil follow her out with a shadow across his gray eyes. When he looked at me, I said, "Country coolie have some big bottom, boy!"

"Resh!" Sunil opened both palms like I was naked and he was trying to cover me then whispered, "You mustn't say them kinda things. That is racist."

"But I am a Indian. If I call another Indian a coolie, how that could be racist? Plus she ass real big. Like a Negro. You sure she not mix?"

"Shhh, Resh." He looked around. The noisy group was leaving so tables and chairs scraped the tile as they were put back.

"Nobody studying we in here. You acting like you never say that. You used to call your own family coolie and laugh. You only here a year and you pick up all them American ways. Every thing is about racism to them. Some Indians are coolies. Plus you didn't hear when she try to insult me first, asking if—"

"We in a public place, Resh. People might get offended. Let we talk about it when we go home, nah. Please." He let out a long breath and his eyes darted around the restaurant, like I was some child misbehaving in public.

I felt like my heart was boiling in my chest. "I tired of this effing shit." I got up and went out the door. I walked toward the sound of cars then stopped to read the street signs because nothing looked familiar in the fading day.

I heard Sunil's voice behind me, calm like none of it happened. "Not that way. Park is this way. You have your Metrocard ready?"

"Yes," my mouth said against my will.

"Home then."

We were getting dressed to go to the Botanic Gardens. Sunil put on the Zegna Jacket over a t-shirt and jeans, and opened the door.

"Where you going?" I was in front the mirror, trying to put my hair in a ponytail.

"To pay the rent. Be right back."

He was gone. The bright day with its car sounds and whistling birds took his place in the doorway. My head throbbed where the black elastic band held it. I took the band out, but the throbbing stayed. I listened between the sounds on Troy Avenue to see if I could hear the exchange between Sunil and the landlady. I thought I was hearing something then a car playing loud music swallowed all the sounds. Barrington Levy's "Living Dangerously" filled up the apartment. It was the remix with Bounty Killer, and Bounty's deep base rounded out Levy's sweetness, warning about all the things that were going to happen to the girl who was living bad. I felt like I wanted to shit and went to the toilet, but nothing happened. I stayed there with the yellow floral dress around my waist and my panties around my ankles until I heard Sunil come back.

"Resh?" he called.

"In here. Coming out now." I got up and flushed.

"You ready?" he asked when I came out. "The ponytail was looking good."

"Yeah, I ready. I was just thinking that the ponytail would be a nice change too." I put my hair up and we left.

"How Mrs. Mannix?" I walked a little behind him along Troy.

"She wasn't home."

I caught up and we held hands. I tried to read the way his hand held mine, how firmly he was holding it, how many fingers were touching me. I studied the pulse in his temple under the skinny gold arm of his aviators. I couldn't read him. He was like a closed fridge. He lifted our hands and touched my cheek with the back of his hand. "Let's take a two-dollar cab to the train station. Ok?"

I nodded, feeling like it was years ago and we were fourteen, going out for the first time. At the corner, he flung out his other arm with a finger pointed, and a dark green Cutlass stopped in front of us.

I had never been to the Brooklyn Gardens. There was some blossom event going on so the place smelled like one big flower and the gardens were separated according to theme like fragrance, herbs, and things like that. The place was crowded, but not so bad that we couldn't walk or anything. There were mostly old White couples who walked and talked slow, and young White families that all looked the same in bright colored expensive clothes that were made to look old, and heavy leather shoes. The moms knelt near the two children to teach at every opportunity, while the dads waited with both hands on the empty double stroller. There were a couple Negro people, young couples on dates and Negro nannies with White kids in strollers.

Sunil went to the bathroom before we left to get lunch at Tom's Restaurant on Washington Avenue. He had left his phone in the bag from the Garden's gift shop and it rang. It was a number from Trinidad so I thought it might be important.

"Hello, this is Sunil phone."

"Hello." His mother had a high-pitched voice.

"Hello, Sunil Mommy."

"Padma?" She asked.

"Mrs. Suinarine, is me…" I was about to say my own name. "Yes, is me, Padma."

"How you? You taking care a Sunny for me?"

"Yes." I put my finger in my other ear to muffle the sounds of the garden.

"How school? You studying hard? Sunny tell me you bright in school."

"Yeah. School going good."

"Good. Good. Where he is? Let me talk to him."

"Oh…He gone out."

"He gone to class?"

"Yeah."

"Ok. You tell he to call me when he come back."

"Yes. I go tell him."

She paused and I heard the TV and people talking in the background. "…He not with she…," she said to someone in the background. "….Padma, I—" I touched the red bar to silence her. Sunil came back just as I ended the call.

"Who call?"

"Your mother."

"I should call she back. Ma don't ever call for nothing." He stepped into the shade to make the call.

"Sunil?"

He looked at me and his eyebrows made a V. "What?" He showed me the phone as in; can't you see I'm doing something?

"How much is your rent?" I had both hands on my hips.

"You know how much it is. You pay it." Lines formed on his forehead.

"I thought you say Mrs. Mannix wasn't home?"

"I thought I could leave my girlfriend in my place and she wouldn't start a CSI investigation?"

"Sunil, you get five thousand a month. You have a set of old clothes. The rent is seven. What you doing with the rest?"

"You and your father want to give me money and tell me how to spend it too? This is some control bullshit. You want receipts? You want pictures of groceries?"

People started to look at us and made big circles as they passed.

"And who really is this Padma? Your ..." I made quotation marks in the air, "Friend. As you say. Your mother—-"

"She is my..." He made quotations too. "Friend." And put the phone in his jacket pocket.

"Sunil. On the phone just now, your mother thought I was Padma and ask she if she was taking care of you. Like if Padma is your woman. I look like a ass to you? I know now Padma is the girl who like you to lick she—"

"Lord." He looked around and held me by one elbow. "It have little children here. Let—-"

"Don't focking touch me!" I walked away.

Outside the metal gates with the leaf pattern, Eastern Parkway was in front of me. I was sweating so I put the handbag on the ground to take off my jacket, and Sunil picked it up.

"Resh. Calm down. Things not how they look."

"How they look, Sunil? I go tell you. You focking that girl and saving my family money to be with she and stay here. Why else you would be saving money? And your mother and them know about it."

"Resh? You—"

"Let me tell you something. If I find out that you and that girl focking, I will fock she up! Because she getting involved in things that don't concern she. Things that in motion long before she bring she big fat coolie ass around." I wanted to tell him that he was mine. But I didn't want to seem hungry.

"Look. You want to go home?"

"Home? I not going back to that place. I going to the hotel where the walls smooth and the windows not covered with dirt. I was forgetting who I was, Sunil, but I remember now."

A couple was getting out of one of those green taxicabs. When they were out, I got in and told the driver I was going to the Soho Grand. I looked back at Sunil, but he was on his phone. Either talking to his mother or who ever. I didn't care. I lay back on the cool seat and tried to think of nothing.

Daddy's friend in the bank said that each month Sunil drew out the money in $500, $500, $500, everyday until it's done. The account had $1002.17, just to keep it open, and to avoid fees. Daddy wasn't checking the statements, because checking up on Sunil was like checking up on me. I didn't tell Daddy about Padma, but after he told me about the withdrawals, he wanted to know why I wanted to know. "No reason," I said. "Was just wondering."

"You sure everything alright?" Daddy asked.

"Yes. Just wondering." What I was really wondering was if Padma had a bank account. But if I asked that favor, they will call Mr. Boodoo and he might get wise and pull the plug. This was my business and I wanted to handle it. I just had to confirm that he was effing that girl. And I could take it from there. So the Monday after the gardens, I texted him and asked him to come over so we could talk.

He came right after class and said how he loved me and that he would never horn me. How I was overacting from stress and that Padma was only a friend. When he mentioned her, I gave him a cut eye and he went back to saying he was sorry and how he wanted to marry me when he returned to Trinidad. I smiled a little bit and said that I loved him too. And he started making Indian dance neck movements, while singing to the tune of "Radica," this soca chutney love song I hated, but he replaced Radica's name with mine, "Love is a secret we have to unravel. If you not with me, I am in trouble. Reshma, why you leave and go? Oooooh, Reshma, why you leave and go..." He could be so nice sometimes.

Later, he was doing the usual and I said, "I want to try what you was trying the last time?"

"What?" He looked a little scared.

I pointed at the place between my legs. "Eat some."

Apparently, he was really, really, really sorry, because he had to wait till I stopped bucking against the bed, until I came back from a strange new place to the calm beige décor with him in it. Then he cupped my flat ass and tuned me over to hit and bite it a few times. Like it was another ass. Kisses covered my body and when he got to my chest, his eyes were closed. He sighed and seemed far away as he rubbed his face against the plain between my bobbies, like if the space between them was soft and fleshy. When he was inside, he moved in odd patterns, not even hearing the noise my belly was making. He gasped from somewhere deep in his chest, like he never did with me, then fell with his face against my neck. He turned onto his back.

"Hmmm. So that is how Padma like to fock?"

His brow seemed to come down over his eyes, like a lintel on an old house. His nostrils flared. He looked at me like he was trying to think of something to say. "Resh..."

"Don't Resh me. I know, you know. You wasn't focking me. You was focking she. Get up and get out."

He rolled onto his stomach. "I don't know what you talking about. You crazy, oui. I tell you I not—-"

"You hear me. Get to fock out!"

He stayed where he was then reached for me with one hand, a smile on his lips. At the same moment, my cell phone rang on the nightstand, a thunderclap in the silent room, and I saw his ass cheeks clench, making an indent at the side and a dimple or two in the smooth pale flesh. I picked up the phone to decline the call then I got on my knees and started hitting Sunil with the flat part of the phone. I hit him in the head and started punching him in the back. He got on his knees and held my hands above my head. He kept saying, "Shhh. Shhh. The people will come to the room." I was screaming and only heard myself then. "Get out," I screamed. "Get Ouuuuuut!"

"I going, I going…" He put on his pants and shoes, and left with his shirt and knapsack in one hand. After he left, I cried with my head resting on knees I had drawn toward my chest. I couldn't stop. My head felt like it would crack open and my stomach hurt. Sobs scraping out of my throat sounded foreign to my ears. It had been a long time. Maybe since my mother died. The shape of Sunil was still on the crisp, white sheets. And I thought about what it would be like to live with only the shape of him, and not him-him. Sunil was the only man I was ever with. Since I was fourteen. "Him, him, him…" I shouted to the empty room. Then I lay on the shape that Sunil had left. I remember crying some more, but I don't remember falling asleep.

On Wednesday, I waited across the street from Pot Stickers, when I knew her class let out. I waited till she and Nadine came out and I crossed the street just as they turned onto the street from the exit. I wrapped my hand in her hair, yanked her head back and slapped her across the face. She screamed, turned around, tried to push me then tried to take her hair out of my hands. Her bag of dumplings and her tote bag of books and papers fell on the ground, the papers blowing all over. Nadine tried to push me away with one hand, the food in the other. "This is none of your focking business!" I palmed her face as I said it and she stepped back. Then Miss Padma got brave and started to push me and tried to grab my hair, but it was tied up under my hat, so

I bent her head back till she lost her balance and kicked her in the back of the knees and she fell in a kneeling position. People started to stop and look, some took out their phones. "What the fock you looking at? Don't feel sorry for she. This coolie bitch focking other people man." I went close to her ear, "You know who you focking with?" I slapped her. "Eh cunt, you know?" I did it again. She nodded. "Answer me, your mother cunt!" I pulled her head back, closer to her heels. Her Adam's apple trembled on her exposed neck as she struggled to breathe.

"Yes," she whispered. Tears fell along the sides of her face and made puddles in her ears.

"No! You don't mother cunt know. Because if you did know, you wouldn't be focking my man. You would know to leave him the fock alone. So let me make you wise." I whispered now, "I am Steven Boodoo daughter and if you come near my focking man again, they will just find your cunt dead in New York," I snapped the fingers on one hand. "And we will wipe out your whole coolie clan in Princes Town. You understand?" I hit her in the face and spread the blood on her cheek from where my ring had cut her. "Answer, Cunt!"

"Yes." The place where her neck met her head beat like a frightened mouse in a sack of brown skin.

"Now, how much money you and Sunil save?"

She widened her eyes.

"How much?" I punched her in the head.

"Thirty." She croaked. "Thirty thou' sah."

"That is my focking money. Draw it out, write a check to me and mail it to Sunil. I know you know where he live. Do it today! You hear me?"

"Yes. My neck."

"Your neck? Your mother cunt!" I let her go. She tried to stand up, one knee on the ground. "This focking coolie girl, playing up in things that don't concern she." I opened my arms and made as if I was going to lunge at her and a small scream escaped her throat. "That is what I thought! Focking Coolie Mother Cunt!"

The students lined the street in small groups. As I walked passed, some lowered their phones and stepped back. When I was clear of them, I hurried to the 6 train on Park.

I was supposed to be in New York for 21 days, but I extended it for another 4 weeks to make all the arrangements. Sunil moved to a nice apartment building near the school, where I could pay the rent with a credit card. And I told Daddy to let me give Sunil his allowance. I cut it to $2000, so he could at least have some cash every month. The day he moved in, I saw Miss Padma by the Jamba Juice. She held her head straight, like she didn't know us. I checked. Sunil didn't even move an eyelash in her direction.

It was the end of June by the time I had to go back. The day before I left, Sunil said he missed home, so I bought a ticket for him and we went back together. In Trinidad, it was just like it was before he left. He stayed with his parents in Princes Town and would sometimes help out in one of the stores then meet me at Club Space on evenings. On Saturdays we partied till late and did Maracas Beach or Tobago on Sundays. One night at the club, the DJ played this boss soca mix with all my favorite songs then Sunil got on the mic and asked me to get married. I said yes and there was a party for us afterwards. Sunil bought a small Astor cut diamond in white gold (I get a bigger one in ten years, of course) with the Padma money.

Me. I gave it to him.

Now everything is in order. In August, after Sunil goes back to New York, I will visit him twice a year and he will visit me. And now that we're engaged, when he visits, he could stay at the mansion in Curepe and nobody will bat an eye. When he's done with the business degree and he's up to scratch, we will get married and he will run a store and probably a club in Central Trinidad, because the nightlife seriously dry in Central. I know what you're thinking. But I have that in check too. If Sunil had a feeling of a feeling that he wanted to try something, the doorman to the building watching everything and will tell me. Plus three years will go by fast and we will be married, a big wedding with gold threads in my sari, the pictures will take up the whole middle section of the *Trinidad Sunday Guardian*. Now that Sunil and me engaged, and even more so when we get married, any woman he's with will be on the outside. But me, I will always be on the inside.

Poor Things

Yvette Benavides

Rita uncoiled a length of twine and looked up at the cloudless April sky. The days were getting warmer and longer, but she still needed a light sweater out in the garden. She held one end of the string and the spool in the other, pulled the garden shears from the back pocket of her jeans, and cut the string flush against the spool. She felt around inside the plastic bag from the Mega-Mart for the small hand-mirror. She pulled the string through the pink plastic handle and joined the two ends. She rolled a small knot with her thumb and index finger, then climbed up to the third step of the ladder leaning against the back gate to hang the mirror on a scraggly peach tree, one in a row of several fruit trees lining the cyclone fence. The branch bowed with the weight of the mirror, and for a second, Rita squeezed her eyes shut against the blinding sun glinting off the mirror.

Picking up the spool, shears, and plastic bag, Rita surveyed her backyard. Every peach, pomegranate, pecan, and mandarin orange tree was like a gaudy Tannenbaum festooned with mirrors and CD disks, shiny crystal beads strung with fishing line like Mardi Gras necklaces.

This would work. She'd read about it online. This was supposed to keep the raptors from invading her property—again. The flashes and shimmers of objects littering the backyard would fend them off and keep them circling high overhead.

Her rooster, Rocky, scratched at the ground next to her black rubber garden boots. She'd never wanted him. He was an accidental rooster. She had purchased four chicks at the feed store. The clerk said they had been sexed. No males. Soon enough, her suspicions were confirmed. She patted Rocky's head. He was clumsy and awkward, with a disproportionately small head and large-breasted body on spindly legs. The golden-laced chickens bullied him at the scratch trough and when she scattered cooked rice or treated them to halved grapes or watermelon. Lucy, the Rhode Island Red, was the real ruler of the roost. She squabbled and squawked and pecked at his face at the trough. He never fought back. The spurs on his legs were useless, like extra toes he'd never use. But he was somehow beautiful, formidable even, with tail feathers so dark blue, they shimmered like black oil. Motionless, he stared at Rita through the black bead eye of his profile. He trailed behind the gaggle of the smallest of the brood, the ones at the bottom of the pecking order—three dappled Sussex hens—to the shade of the mesquite. *Otro pobrecito*, thought Rita, shaking her head. She decided she would worry most about him when the hawks returned.

She looked out in the distance at the trucks, earthmovers and cranes. Concrete columns stretched up and up, thirty feet into the sky, marring the horizon and impeding her view of the Carrizo-lined river.

In those infrequent lulls, when the machines weren't going at full throttle, in the distance, she could hear the tinny din of a Spanish-language radio station and the men's voices, one distinct from the next. They arrived early in the morning, the trucks pulling up slowly. When they departed at 4:00 in the afternoon, the trucks screeched and kicked up gravel and dust. Even when they were packing up at the end of the day, the men shouted to each other over the phantom cacophony and chaos.

Maybe all the noise and commotion of the trucks and the men had scared the predators right out of their normal river routes and on to other victims. The understory of the canopy of willows and mesquite trees by the river offered protection from the hawks. But Rita had noted the rookeries of egrets and heron were less populated over the last several weeks. And the erection of the border wall had certainly had an effect on the people of Pobrecito, who had signed petitions, scheduled town hall meetings, and developed a kind of collective hope that their efforts could bring about a change.

Rita wasn't born in Pobrecito, but had lived here long enough to know that it took a lot for the pobrecitos to pull together. She had seen it happen only once before over the years.

The first time they had come together was after the first murder: Elena. After the funeral, they convened in the small community center next to Our Lady of Sorrows Catholic Church. The usual back-slapping career politicians postured and held forth and called for swift justice. Each speaker was rotund, mustachioed, and under-dressed for the funeral in their ample guayaberas. She knew each man only by his undignified nickname. Even their campaign signs didn't include their real first names: "Vote! Wawi Sanchez for Justice of the Peace," "Chilo Villarreal for Mayor," and "El Moco Rodriguez for County Commissioner."

Rita had been hungover when she arrived at the funeral mass. Because she was an outsider, a teacher, and considered attractive, the people of the town treated her like a celebrity—maybe a second-rate one, a telenovela extra—not the fair-skinned, hazel-eyed blondes of the myopic studio system that corruptly monopolized the industry.

The news of the murder had sent Rita straight to the cabinet under her kitchen sink where behind the dish soap, Brillo pads and Ajax, she kept bottles of booze—rum, tequila, gin, brandy and bourbon, a few bottles of a cheap wine she liked. She liked having a surplus of bottles. Full and unopened, they looked like giant glittering gems. But soon enough, they stared back at her, half-empty and horrible at their places on her nightstand or the coffee table, or on the ledge of the tub. The night she heard about the murder, she sat on the kitchen floor and finished off a bottle of Malbec right down to that familiar empty ugliness.

When she entered the church the next morning, the smell of incense, bad breath and cheap perfume made her swoon. She knew she had to walk all the way to the steps before the altar to pay her respects, to see the faces of Elena's parents and the little brother, Betito, who didn't betray his emotions. And then she would have to stand before the casket. She would have to look into Elena's face. Elena. Her student. Her favorite student, if she was going to be honest about it. She was a good writer and capable of succeeding in college—qualities so rare among the pobrecitos. Rita encouraged her to plan for that eventuality, for scholarships and homesickness and working twice as hard as the other students from better high schools.

There they were. Rita had come to expect to see the cadre of Maria Magdalenas at most public occasions. They were a group of busy-bodies, known not for being reformed women of ill repute like their namesake, but for their ability to cry. They were fixtures at every funeral, wedding, baptism and First Holy Communion. Their job was to weep melodramatically, almost as if on cue. They instinctively synchronized whimpers and wails and choreographed and conducted the rest of the churchgoers and made each event suitably dramatic, even at the happy occasion of a quinceañera.

The quinceañera. Elena's quinceañera. Rita hadn't wanted to attend. Out of the cocoon of the classroom, there were no rules. She wasn't in charge. She would be in her civilian clothes, not her usual conservative uniform of black polyester pants and floral print blouses. She looked forward to her Saturday nights after a long week at the school and a long day of working in the garden, cleaning house or grading. She'd lie on the couch and channel-surf and drink. Sometimes, after a couple of drinks, she called QVC to order clothes and make-up featured on the shopping channel. There weren't many clothing stores in Pobrecito. The small mall in the center of town housed a chiropractor's office, an arcade, a hobby shop, and a single department store. Rita had been a clotheshorse before moving to Pobrecito. She was obsessed with clothes and accumulating shoes and boots and lingerie. She'd awaken the next day with the phone on her chest trying to recall the conversation of the night before with the QVC operator.

There would be booze at the quinceañera. This was Pobrecito, Texas. Beer and tequila were as ubiquitous as water at family gatherings—even baptismal or First Holy Communion receptions. But she would not imbibe in front of the students. As far as they were concerned she was a teetotaler who didn't know the difference between añejo and reposado. In the community center next to Our Lady of Sorrows Catholic Church where Father Tom, the Polish priest with a penchant for Dr. Pepper, had blessed her during a solemn mass with the priest's incongruous homily and message to the young girl about the fifteenth birthday being the threshold to womanhood. How this debut was a sign to society that she was ready to be married and wouldn't any young man want to be with her. "Not 'wit' ju," he said, making air quotes, "you know 'wit' ju," his hyper-awareness of his poor English tripping his tongue.

People in the pews fidgeted. Here and there an old woman would conspicuously and exaggeratedly shake her head, and the men would look down at their hands on their laps.

Elena dissembled, smiling and nodding at the priest. Families invest as much money and effort for a quinceañera as they do for a wedding. But Elena's was simple. Her parents were modest people—her mother a homemaker and seamstress, her father a truck driver. They had been migrant workers, too, just like Rita and her family. But Rita never shared that part of her life with anyone.

Elena's mother had made the quinceañera dress herself—a baby pink sateen with tulle overlay and tiny white rose embellishments all over the bodice. Elena was every bit the princess in that dress with her shoulder-length hair in loose curls, a tiny rhinestone clip to hold back her bangs.

Rita had always thought that Elena admired her and that she did well in English class because she wanted to please her teacher. When Elena saw her at the reception in the community center, her face lit up. She ran toward Rita and hugged her tightly.

Rita sat at a table with Fr. Tom and Doña Delia. That was an odd pairing. Delia operated a small beauty shop out of the front room of her house, but she was also a curandera and customers either went to her for a haircut or a cure—for evil eye, to ward off gossip, to make a wayward mate return. The loud music meant Rita didn't have to talk to anybody. She gave her back to the priest and the curandera and watched the kids dancing and gyrating unabashedly to the nasty reggaeton songs she despised. Still, the misogynistic lyrics and repetitive melodies were somehow easier for her to handle than small talk.

Ardilla and Araña approached the table. She had never been their teacher, didn't know if the two had ever even gone to high school, but they were always around, whizzing past on a skateboard—even Araña. She wanted to be invisible. Araña was shy, but Ardilla was talkative and tended to stand in your personal space. They were cousins, each one abandoned by his mother. One sister had met a man in the cotton fields of Cotulla, Texas. Ardilla went to live with his grandmother, Chela. The other sister had abandoned Araña. The story Rita had heard at Delia's was that he had been a blue baby and his mother left him because her new man did not want to take in a boy who would have such special needs and require potentially expensive medical care. Little did he know, the baby would live beyond adolescence—even without any therapies or curative interventions. His legs were withered. He walked on his hands and knees, dragging the dead weight of the legs behind him.

He wore kneepads and wrestler's gloves. The unsightly legs were always covered by his frayed, faded jeans. She'd heard his feet were gnarled, all long toes fused together and resembling a larger version of the pointy claw-like feet of a spider.

The two boys joined the young people on the dance floor. Araña remained on the fringes of the space and bobbed his head in time with the music. Ardilla danced wildly and waved him over. The other kids did, too. Rita smiled in spite of herself.

When the dance evolved into the expected quinceañera rituals of the father-daughter dance, the presentation of the last doll, and the exchanging of the little-girl flats for a pair of high heels, Rita took her leave without saying goodbye to anyone. She could see Elena and her father dancing. For such a shy, quiet man, Mr. Perez certainly could dance. Elena beamed at him. Rita could see they were both smiling and crying at once.

The next time she saw Elena, she was in the casket in front of the church altar. She was wearing the same baby pink sateen dress with the tulle overlay and tiny white roses embroidered all over the bodice.

Rita had pulled the grunting weight of the chicken tractor underneath the gnarled mesquite tree that seemed to be taking a bow. In its shade, the chickens would be safe from the red-tailed hawks.

She hadn't wanted to move it, but three days ago, when she had stepped out into the cool afternoon, she saw something red. In that split second, the flash of color was pleasing. Red and white were the school colors at Pobrecito High School. She refused to wear the apple red school polo shirt teachers were required to wear on pep rally days. When the state cut the funding for athletic programs, she didn't have to fight that battle anymore. She was always on the outside—more pobre than any other pobrecito.

Red. She recognized her reaction to the color and her surprise at her own wistful response to it. But then, just feet from the backdoor a hawk pecked in spastic, apoplectic, head-jerking motions at what had been Nutmeg, the shyest chicken—a golden-laced Wyandotte. The hawk seemed enormous, like a grown man, a giant, a murderer, hunched over its small, young cannibalized victim. But it was a female bird. Rita knew that. Startled, Rita felt her breath go out of her body, and a sinking hollowness replaced it. Impulsively, she ran out, clapped her hands, then waved them wildly in front of her and screamed, "Get out of here!" The hawk stared back, unmoving, its eyes penetrating and knowing. Rita felt that it could see inside her pounding heart. She looked away to see another hawk perched on the cyclone fence that separated her property from the dirt levee and, just beyond, the banks of the river, the men and their cranes, trucks, and earthmovers. That hawk seemed smaller, somehow dumber. That was the male, thought Rita. She always felt stronger around someone dumb. She grabbed a rake leaning against the back wall of her house. She heard a beating of wings and both hawks flew straight up like helicopters into the still, golden air. Rita focused on the red tails flared like fans. The hawks extended their wings, gliding in stone silence until it hurt her eyes to keep looking, keep trying to see or understand what had just devastated her small world.

Nutmeg's small fist-sized head lay bloodied in the compost bed. The hens liked to forage there and peck at strawberry hulls or egg shells or other scraps she scraped off her plate or skillet. Nutmeg was easy prey there for the hawk that must have pulled her body out of the bed, perhaps to carry the bloodied body away. Instead the hawk gutted her there. The spray of bloody, muddy feathers and then the sight of three more hawks flying overhead told Rita that they had been complicit in the murder and they would be back.

The flash of red. The school colors of Pobrecito High School.

Rita had arrived on campus early on that day—like every other day. The color red was everywhere—the lockers, accent walls, dusty school pennants. And there. There in her classroom. Smears on the floor that led to the body of the young girl. The good girl. The favorite. Slumped in the corner.

The small garden statue of St. Francis holding out a bowl that Rita filled with water for the house finches, sparrows, blue jays, and cardinals watched as Rita dug a hole next to the other tiny graves marked with river stones. He had been a mute witness to Nutmeg's attack, but also to the many funerals of other creatures Rita had lost over the years since she'd first moved to Pobrecito. She thought that Jesus and all his saints were deaf and insensible to her old petitions, but she sometimes felt like talking to the statue. Besides the chickens, he was her sole companion while she labored at the many hoop-housed garden beds of vegetables. She fretted over the beds of tomato plants, collard greens, lettuces, cabbage, broccoli, green beans, radishes, and all types of herbs. The hawks weren't the least interested in the large heirloom tomatoes, their conspicuous color and size peeking out from their metal cages and tangles of sticky stems and leaves.

The hole was deep and the width of the shoebox where she put the parts of Nutmeg the hawks had left behind. Scavenging for them was a grisly business. She had taken to putting a kitchen cloth in each tiny sepulcher. Her father had started that practice in the apple orchards of Michigan where Rita had traveled for years as a child and teen with her parents and sister. One day, she found a tiny white mewling kitten. Day after day, he was underfoot. Rita's sister was mentally disabled. She had never been diagnosed, but might be considered severely autistic. She was mute and couldn't do much for herself. She didn't help in the fields, but spent her time sitting, rocking back and forth, in their father's truck. Rita let her play with the kitten while she returned to her place in the cucumber fields. Cucumbers were covered in hair-fine thorns. They didn't hurt or penetrate the skin, but she hated that work. At the end of the day, Rita and her parents returned to the truck. Rita could see Marina rocking back and forth. Rita opened the door to take her kitten. "Where is my kitty, Marina?" She moved Marina's feet roughly to search the floor. She pulled at her sister's big, doughy body, pulled her out of the truck. Marina fell to the ground, a dog's howl coming from her mouth as their mother ran to the girl. On the seat of the truck where Marina had been sitting was the white kitten. In that large dimple where Marina had been sitting, the kitten lay as if curled up and sleeping. With the lightest finger-grip, Rita lifted him up. His head fell slack, a dribble of bright red blood marred the pure whiteness of his fur.

Rita's father went along with her mother's plan to bury the kitten after nightfall. Furtively, worried the patrón would see him, he labored to dig the hole next to an apple tree. Rita watched from the truck as he took his blue bandana from his back pocket to wipe the sweat on his face and the back of his neck. But, instead he shook it out over the kitten and gently placed it in the hole. Rita cried. Marina laughed into the air and rocked.

Rita gently dropped the shoebox with Nutmeg's remains wrapped in a kitchen towel in the hole by St. Francis. She moved the dirt with her hands and filled the hole. She took a river rock from the small mound of them by the statue. The graves of a baby mourning dove that had fallen from the nest during a storm, an ant-filled crow she'd found under the nogal one morning, and a small stray dog someone had run over down the street from her house, all dotted the small space.

Rita saw a flash of baby pink—the rose bush by the statue. That pink. Like the pink sateen. She hadn't expected such emotion at the girl's casket. She turned to face the family sitting in the front pew. Mr. Perez looked straight ahead, his lips quivering. Mrs. Perez in a black dress stared straight ahead. She looked dead herself, and then she slumped down in the pew like a sack of flour. Rita's impulse was to look away. To run away. She pitched forward before the casket and landed at the feet of the statue of San Martín de Porres. Where was his broom? That is all she remembered. That and coming to and seeing the faces of the pobrecitos— of Betito—somehow impassive and compassionate at once—Ardilla, his narrow face and his buck teeth, and Araña closest in eye-level to Rita because he was on his hands and knees.

Rita turned on the hose, wet her hands and wiped them on her jeans. She filled the large waterer for the chickens. They were unwieldy contraptions, but they had to be filled daily.

She looked across the way at the men and the trucks and the first part of what would be the wall to separate two countries. Then she saw Ardilla and Araña. She hadn't seen them out here in a long time, since the first arrival of those trucks weeks before. Ardilla carried his fishing gear and Araña followed close behind. *Pobrecito*, thought Rita. He moved like a human metronome walking on his hands, dragging the dead legs behind him. She heard the shouts of men. Laughter. She could see Ardilla drop his gear and lunge at one of the men. The other men surrounded Araña. Rita screamed at them to stop. They must have heard her faintly, seen the glittering objects hanging on the trees. The men got in their trucks and sped away leaving Ardilla and Araña to a momentary freedom by the river where they would fish as they always had before.

At this safe distance, there alone in her garden, Rita felt the breath go right out of her body. She didn't run to the kitchen cabinet to her stash of alcohol. Sober, staring out into the expanse of what she could see of the land and the river and two of Elena's friends, she sobbed and let herself cry. She recalled the sight of them among the other pallbearers at the funeral. How had Araña managed it? It was just a matter of course for the pobrecitos to include him in the solemn procession. The men, some dressed in guayaberas, others in polyester, plaid, outdated sport coats, held the handles on the sides of the casket down low as if together they carried a heavy suitcase. In that configuration, Araña could join them in shouldering the weight. She noted his denim jacket and thought that might be his Sunday best. Las Maria Magdalenas looked on, shaking their heads, pressing balled up tissues to their open eyes, and muttering, "Pobrecito."

Rita shuddered and sniffed. She searched the face of St. Francis, straightened up, and then wiped her eyes roughly with the back of her hand. She looked up to see six hawks flying overhead in a circle. She swore under her breath, never taking her eyes off them, her heart pounding. She looked around searchingly. The hens were in the shade of the mesquite by the chicken tractor. Rocky would be there, too, watching through those fixed black beads.

The hawks seemed to disappear and then would reappear again. She could hear the screeches of a mockingbird protecting her nest of fledglings from their silent threats. She moved the hose from one waterer to the next one, never moving her skyward gaze. She rubbed the back of her neck and closed her eyes to rest them.

The beating and rustle of feathers was all she heard before the shriek. Rita fell backwards against the small, scraggly peach tree. She could feel the blood, warm and feather-light on her lip, the cold muddy water pooling around her bottom and her legs. The sight of Elena sitting in a puddle of dark red blood in the corner of the empty classroom flashed in her mind. Her own reflection in the pink hand mirror came in and out of view as it dangled before her on its string. She saw over and again the deep gouge across her cheek. She pulled the mirror and its noose slipped off the tree. She squeezed her eyes shut and opened them to see the rooster stretching up. His legs looked longer by inches. He beat his wings and crowed. She could see the blood on his spur.

The Eternal Pursuit of the Whale's Song

Keya Mitra

My fiancé Simon, my mother, and I boarded Air Hawaii from the Houston Intercontinental Airport around seven in the morning to visit my dying father. My mother, who came from a traditional Indian family, had still refused to grant my father a divorce even though she hadn't spoken to him since he'd retired a decade earlier from his engineering firm and moved to Honolulu. His assistant Emily—his only companion—was the one who called to tell us that my father was on his way out. But, always the dutiful wife, my mother booked a flight immediately. When I questioned the decision, she just kept repeating herself to avoid further argument. This was her M.O. "He's my husband," she said. "My *husband*. My husband."

"Yes," I said. "And it's insane to pretend you have a relationship with him. *Insane. Insane.*"

On the plane my mother sat herself between Simon and me. Her phobia of being peripheral was worse than her fear of death.

Simon hated my mother but hated confrontation even more, so he promptly fell asleep. I pinched his arm. His head bobbed, and his eyes flickered open. Then he drooled on my hand.

"Wake up," I hissed. We'd been dating for six months, engaged for three, and lately he'd been driving me crazy with his constant state of robotic calm. Even when he was awake he seemed half-asleep. Lately sex between us seemed meticulously planned (Simon was a mathematician).

The motion of our lovemaking was like a see-saw, a steady up and down motion with little variation other than the occasional change in positioning. Did he stay up nights figuring out the intricate calculus of orgasm?

My mother lifted the armrest between us. Boundaries aggravated her, and she dispensed of them whenever possible. "Have the two of you talked about babies?" she asked.

"No," I said wearily. "We're not even *married*."

She clasped her hands together. "Every day, Leela," she said. "I pray every day." Then: "My mother didn't marry until she was twenty-six. Your age. She thought she had plenty of time. But then—poof! Her eggs dried up and her life was over."

"There was no poof," I said. "She had you, and she lived until she was 75."

"Oh, there was a poof all right," she said. "She wanted six kids and ended up with one."

She tucked my bra strap under my shirt. I'd been raised to think that God was always just around the corner with his Polaroid, ready to snap the picture that would be put to the committee on Judgment Day. If your bra strap or underwear ever made an appearance, that was it for you.

The groggy morning light strained to fill the plane. It was soporific, engulfing us like a giant yawn. My mother's wedding ring glinted in the sunlight. I hadn't seen it in years. It had become part of the tangle of jewelry in a drawer that had come to resemble a junkyard.

"Why are you wearing that?" I asked. "Oh right. It's your wedding ring. Your *wedding ring*."

She closed her eyes with a melodramatic sigh. A few minutes later, a tortoise-necked man on my other side began talking to us.

"Are you two on vacation?" The man asked.

My mother missed no opportunity to flaunt her tragedies. Her eyes flickered open. "No," my mother said, "my husband is *dying*."

He murmured his apologies, paused, then said: "Your husband sure was lucky to have such a gorgeous wife." I rolled my eyes.

My mother bowed her head. She wore a white button down shirt and pants, a loose outfit that seemed a slap in the face to the gorgeous tautness of her body. For her, any display of sexuality had to be entirely accidental; when someone complimented her on her shirt, she'd notice a "button she'd missed." Sexual suggestiveness was like shoplifting; it seemed to thrill her, but when confronted she denied it had been intentional.

But, even though she was all too aware of her beauty—which the smitten described as "exceptional" and the envious, like me, "fucking unjust"—she wore her loveliness like a kid given a necklace of pure gold. She was uneasy possessing it even as she reveled in its value to the outside world.

She was a pharmacist, and I began working alongside her as a pharmacy technician two years ago, just after graduating from the University of Houston. She couldn't bear to be alone after my father moved, so I took the job to be near her. When I was a child, my mother told me that she had pursued pharmacy to help people heal and to carry on the legacy of her father, a doctor in Kolkata who'd treated many of his poorer customers for free. But she tended to be sympathetic to only the most "appropriate" conditions and illnesses. Influenza was acceptable; gonorrhea was absolutely not.

But my mother's loveliness duped others into deeming her a saint. One customer at the pharmacy referred to her as a "Hot Mother Teresa," especially once he heard that she was nursing an ailing husband. My father was diagnosed with Multiple Sclerosis in his twenties and by his early forties had been confined to a wheelchair. After he got sick, my father grew immune to my mother's charms and to the charms of the world around him. He stopped speaking unless absolutely necessary.

Around him Mom constantly clamored to make noise, trying to make herself heard. Even after my father disappeared from our lives, she never lost the habit of seeking attention.

The next hour and a half consisted of my bearing witness to Mom's grotesque flirtation with Turtle Man. I tried to shake Simon awake; he rewarded me with more spittle. So I tapped my mother on the knee. "Switch seats with me." She didn't put up a fight; now that she had Turtle's attention, I was off the hook for a while.

Simon's hair was strewn carelessly over his eyes. The near perfection of his nose, combined with the sharpness of his cheekbones, created the illusion of arrogance. I'd fallen for him in part because of his name—I'd had a crush on Simon Le Bon from Duran Duran for years, and the fact that my Simon resembled the lead singer (aside from being Indian) seemed too much of a coincidence for me to ignore.

Comfortably seated next to Simon, I sang Duran Duran's "My Name is Rio" into his ear until he couldn't fake sleep any longer. "You win," he said after attempting to drool on me a few more times. He grabbed my hand, kissing it briefly. "But you better be carrying Xanax on you. You realize that the FDA approved it after meeting your mother."

My fingers slid into his. His hands were beautiful and soft.

I'd met Simon at the pharmacy several months earlier. My mother's eyes scanned his body when he walked in. He had all the prerequisites—Indian, with a good build, no evident piercings. As he slid a prescription to my mother, she glanced at it, wagged a finger at him, and said, "Yes! I *knew* I'd seen you before."

"I'm sorry," he said, shoving his hands into his pockets. "I don't think we've met—"

"Years ago," she insisted. "You used to build Lego castles with my daughter Leela. We spent some time with your family when the two of you were children."

I was filling an order at the time. "I don't remember ever building a Lego castle, Mom," I called out.

"You spent *hours* building Lego castles," she said. She stepped back, grabbed my sleeve, and guided me to the counter. "Leela here stole my bindis and put them all over her face and told you that she had a rare strand of Monster Pox. You were so scared of her, Simon. You ran around the house screaming *Monster Pox, Monster Pox*."

According to my mother, I'd coincidentally had childhood friendships with several Indian males (always in their twenties) who'd walked into the pharmacy.

A new customer approached my mother, and I took the opportunity to whisper to Simon: "I'm sorry. She's totally lying. We never built Lego castles together. My mother scares me sometimes."

He laughed. "*Pharmacists* scare me."

"Why?"

"You have my life in that computer," he said. "A prescription can be as intimate as a diary. You could write a whole book about me if you wanted."

"Right," I said, "because you're *that* interesting." He grinned. And I began to feel an intense attraction to everything about this man I didn't know.

Two days later, he came in with a prescription for Cipro and a reservation at an Italian restaurant for the following night.

Our flight landed at 5:02 p.m. My mother called Emily on the cab ride to the hotel. The woman said that my father had died at approximately 4:32 p.m., which sounded like no approximation at all, and my mother hung up and stared at Simon and me like a bird that had just slammed into a glass window.

We were staying at the Royal Hawaiian, a pink palace overlooking Waikiki Beach. Though my father never spoke to us again after he left, he sent my mother checks without fail every month, so she was as rich as she was miserable. As we passed through the lobby, a man and woman were taking their vows, impeccably dressed and holding hands like figurines you'd see on a wedding cake. The view was beautiful, but the wedding seemed zoo-like. Strangers wearing sand-coated flip-flops and swimsuits stopped and gawked. Then they kept walking, talking loudly.

The room Simon and I were sharing had the pink sheen of the rest of the palace. It had a large balcony and windows, and the splashes and screeches and warmth outside flooded our room. I stretched out on the bed. In the fullness of the sunlight my stomach seemed more sensual in its softness. Everything was new. I pulled at Simon's pants, and he turned around.

I winked at him.

"Honey, your dad just died."

"I haven't seen him in ten years," I said. "There's no need for me to go celibate."

He sat beside me on the bed and gazed out the window. "But he was your father."

I'd told Simon about Dad—about how in his early twenties he'd been training to run in the Olympics when he was diagnosed with MS. After that, he self-medicated to tolerate the gradual wasting away of his body. But I hadn't told Simon about the last time I visited Kolkata with my parents, when I was eleven. I told him about the visit now, about how my father's pendulous stomach flattened within the first fourteen days of our visit, and the heaviness of his eyes diminished for some time. In his childhood Dad made his own fighter kites out of bamboo sticks and rice paper, and he laid them out for me on his childhood bed like a shy kindergartener. The colors were bold—purple, blue, red—and I could see the kites had been made in spurts of exhilaration, in the midst of a vision of himself as a creator, an innovator. The tissue was poorly pasted and torn. I pointed this out, and he said: "Well, I was only a boy when I made them," he said. I had never imagined my father as a boy. I had to close my eyes and picture him, a child, inhabiting this strange house years ago.

When he asked me if I wanted to fly the kites, I saw the child in my father once again—his joy, pure and unfiltered, shone in his eyes. That was what I'd loved about Simon too. The childlike glee in his eyes.

"The kites you see in America are mostly for decorative purposes," he told me during our first lesson on the roof. He'd limped as he climbed the stairs up to the roof, but, once seated, he sat tall in his chair. "But these kites are alive; they have a mind of their own. They're called fighter kites for a reason; the goal is to cut other people's strings until your kite is the only one remaining."

The roof of my grandparents' home was concrete and flat. My father handed me a reel wound with a thin, transparent string made out of ground glue and glass. When he first mentioned flying kites, I fantasized he would burst into song like the father in *Mary Poppins*.

There was no singing, but my father was almost giddy as he freed his kite into the air and showed me how to release mine. My kite was defiant, delinquent, darting around in all directions. My father, on the other hand, was a puppeteer on an inverted stage; the kite's motions corresponded perfectly with the movement of my father's hands. His kite swooped in and cut mine, swiftly, gracefully, before sailing on.

At the end of the lesson he commanded: "Now cut mine." His kite was suspended, paralyzed, in the sky—an open target. With its wings spread apart, it looked like a victim of sacrifice as I fumbled with my reel. It bobbed patiently in the air like a martyr, in acceptance of its approaching death. It took several attempts, but I finally managed to sever the string in choppy, amateur movements. And then I burst into tears. Dad blinked, startled. Then he wrapped me in an awkward embrace. "It's just part of it, Leela. One kite has to lose."

Simon nodded, listening. "But you didn't want to win."

"It was something he'd made, Simon. That he made as a boy. And it was lost to the sky."

Simon smoothed back my hair, pulling my face to his torso. The gentleness of his touch still moved me. "Maybe he was trying to teach you something about saying goodbye."

"Well, duh. But I didn't want to say goodbye," I said. My face was pressed against his shirt, and I heard the petulance in my voice.

"Of course you didn't, baby," Simon said softly. Then he stepped back. "I'm going to get some fishing equipment while it's still light out," he said with a faint smile, "but I'll be back."

"You're going to leave me alone with her?"

"How about this," he said, his smile strained. "I'll bring you back a nice long rod."

"You better," I said. "I haven't seen a rod in a while."

I watched from the balcony as Simon made his way down the beach, his shoulders hunched. As handsome as he was, his posture was terrible. I imagined him as a kid, small and ill at ease with his body, and some of my warmth for him returned.

In the beginning, our love had been dizzying. On our first date, he blurted out, "You have beautiful arms."

"That I've never heard before," I laughed. I had been wearing a red strapless dress and worried all evening that my breasts were sprawled over the table on exhibition for all to see.

"Oh yeah," he responded. "They make me think of trees—tall, happy trees with the branches hanging over the water. They're lovely. Powerful."

"That makes absolutely no sense, weirdo," I said, laughing. But, as nonsensical as it was, the compliment roused me—it introduced the possibility of something surprising and real.

Over the next few weeks we groped one another with the desperation of teenagers breaking curfews; defying the idea of the austere match our parents thought they'd made. We violated their ideals in our secret moments—sex in Memorial Park behind a scrawny cluster of trees barely separating us from the passing joggers, crude verbal exchanges during love-making. I still lived with my mother, and our sexual trysts seemed a delicious contradiction to her outdated values.

"I might be starting to love you, Indian Simon Le Bon," I whispered one night as we groped in the parking lot outside a Kroger's.

"Then marry me, Indian Natalie Portman," he murmured, his breath warm against my ear.

It struck me months later that we'd essentially committed to marrying avatars, not real people. But I figured, back then, that engagement would naturally lead to emotional intimacy. Of course, it didn't. We'd reveled in deceiving our parents for so long, but once we had their approval we were left with our unformed selves. And soon our relationship became one long conversational pause—with pressure to speak, though nothing remained to be said.

I grabbed a blanket and settled into a chair on the balcony. Surfers skated over the frothy waves below. Off in the distance three naked men played soccer, kicking the ball as their genitals jumped around like pom-poms. I squinted, wishing I'd brought my binoculars. It had been weeks since I'd seen genitals—from near or afar.

My mother opened the hotel room with the spare key—of course she'd insisted on taking it—and sat down on the balcony. "Where's Simon?"

"Down at the beach."

She looked vaguely alarmed. "Without you?" She peered at the Pom-Pom genital boys on the beach. "Are those boys naked?"

I held up a hand. "What did you find out about Dad?"

"Your father wanted his body cremated," she said. "No funeral. I'm going now to see him. He's been moved to the funeral home. Do you want to come?"

I nodded—I had to—though the idea of greeting his corpse nauseated me.

She wiped her eyes with the side of her hand. "Your father must have loved it here."

He would have loved it. The vast expanse of sand. The openness of the sky.

During the last few weeks of our visit to Kolkata, my uncles flew their kites with my father, and the volume of conversation rose as their kites approached one another, dodged, and then attacked. My cousins, who were watching, roared like sports commentators, lauding or dismissing the kites. "That kite has no balls!" One cousin heckled. "It doesn't deserve to be black. It should be wearing a pink, frilly dress."

Gradually the kites acquired personalities—my father's kite, Obi-Wan Kenobi from *Star Wars*, was the meditative type. My oldest uncle's kite, named Fonzie after the *Happy Days* character, was overconfident—a self-assured teenager challenging the older virtuoso. When my father severed my uncle's kite, it wasn't without some sadness that we watched Fonzie float out of sight. Sure he was brash and pompous—but he was young, and he'd made a valiant effort. My father initially bristled with irritation when my uncles heckled him, but eventually he softened, unable to contain his laughter. It broke free with startling force, and my mother gaped at him. *Did you just laugh?* She asked. *My God, the sky must be falling!*

But underneath her mocking tone resided a deep, intimate respect. She would sit next to me and gaze reverently at my father like he was a prophet. It was easy during those moments to see how it had been different once between them, and the faint breeze around us was light with optimism, a hopefulness that faded soon after we returned to Houston. Soon after that trip he was confined to a wheelchair.

My mother rose from her seat on the balcony, and I followed her outside. She clutched her purse with both hands, as though it was in danger of being swept away by the wind. I held her hand as we waited for a cab.

Inside the casket my father's body was small and doll-like, his face almost shriveled. He was dressed in a white shirt buttoned to the collar. His fingers were splayed, his hands flat on his chest. I wanted to put something in his hands to bridge the vast, lonely space between them.

A year after we got back from India, my father and I went to the park to fly kites. My father hadn't gotten used to his wheelchair, and his movements were jerky, frustrated. The kites moved groggily through the sky. "It's this damn heat," he grumbled, swatting at the air.

"But it was even hotter in India," I said timidly. He said nothing. His kite had become lodged in an oak tree. I stood up to retrieve it, but he put a hand on my wrist to restrain me and wheeled himself over to the tree. He tried to stand and yank on the string, but he fell back into the chair with a thud.

My parents argued in their bedroom for hours after we returned. When it quieted I found my mother in the kitchen, staring into a glass of water. "He used to make magic," she said. "He refuses to even try anymore. He'll barely even talk to me."

I was silent, the marble floor cold beneath my feet. The month before he left us, my father passed his days in bed, staring blankly at the ceiling. I brought him his meals upstairs, and every time I came close to his motionless body I was terrified of finding a stiff corpse. I watched his belly, silently praying for it to rise. It always did, but my relief was short-lived. I mentally prepared for his death daily. Was happiness like food? I wondered. Once deprived of it for too long, would Dad eventually die?

The morning he left us for good, he wheeled himself to my bed and hugged me. My feet were bare, and at that moment I badly wanted a pair of socks. I was exposed, unprotected, without them. "My precious girl," he said, his head heavy on my shoulder. "I wish I could stand it, the wasting away of my body, my spirit. I wish I was vulnerable enough to let you watch it happen." His voice was hoarse, and when he let go my shoulder was damp from his tears. "Because you are so dear to me."

I said nothing. He'd left, in spirit, long ago. I watched him wheel himself out of my room, slumped in his chair. Nothing remained to attach him to the world.

My mother wept at my side. Emily stood quietly in a corner. She had organized his life after he moved to Hawaii, enabling him to live in virtual isolation. She was the conduit between him and the outside world: getting his groceries, making his phone calls, emptying his bedpan. Her demeanor was stiff, unobtrusive, asexual—everything my father would have wanted from an employee.

I couldn't cry. My father had taught me to sever ties with him that day I cut his kite and watched it disappear into the sky. I could have mourned at a ceremony, dressed in somber grey tones. There I could slip in and out of sadness as though it was a rented suit. But there was no funeral here, no collective grieving. There was only a body as still in death as it had been in life.

After we'd visited India for the last time, my paternal grandparents passed away, and my father's childhood home was sold. He'd only brought with him two kites—one of which we'd abandoned in the tree. The afternoon my father left us, I raced to the park on my bike, praying that the kite was still intact, securely tethered to the tree. But all that remained was a scrap of pink tissue dangling from a branch.

My mother virtually charged into Emily, hugging her tightly. "We were so in love. Did he talk about me often?"

Emily threw a desperate glance in my direction. *Tell the truth*, I thought. *Please.*

Emily looked away. "He spoke of you so fondly."

In the cab on the way back to the hotel my mother was still wailing. "Did you hear that? We were in love. *Emily* said. Emily *said*."

I sighed and took her hand in mine. "I made reservations for us all to go snorkeling tomorrow morning. It'll take our mind off all this."

She sniffed. "We came to mourn. Not take a vacation."

"Stay at the hotel then and mourn," I said. "But grieving isn't a full time job. I need a distraction."

She didn't respond, and I knew she would come. Since my father had left us, she'd grown terrified of being unseen for too long. Even mourning had to be a group-activity.

I returned to my hotel room alone. The sun still lingered in the sky—a dazzling orange, it appeared to rise from the sea like smoke. It was hard to imagine it was making its descent. The bustle below had quieted to a low rumble of voices. A man walked alone by the ocean, which surged and retreated from the banks in a self-assured rhythm. A steady accumulation of murmurs came from a party inside a giant red tent parked perilously close to the ocean. The red flap floundered in the wind whenever a new couple entered.

My relationship with Simon deteriorated soon after we became a real couple. Shortly after our engagement, we spent the night together, and Simon began talking dirty in Bengali. I didn't have a clue what he was saying. My parents had planned on teaching me Bengali, but each held the other responsible for teaching me the language. So I never learned. Simon continued his crude Bengali monologue, and finally I said: "I'm sorry. I can only talk dirty in English."

"You don't speak Bengali?"

"No," I said, breathing on his neck, "but I can be more crass and inventive in English than you could ever imagine."

"Well, that's even better," he said, grabbing me. But he was more distant that night, and I felt like a felon. The awkwardness between us never went away. When Simon's parents called and he lapsed into long conversations in Bengali, I'd sneak away to the backyard, away from his laughter and warm words.

I changed into my flip-flops and bathing suit, seized by a need to shake myself out of chronic weariness. I grabbed a flashlight and then went downstairs. The air near the beach was chilly, and my throat was dry as I slogged through the wet sand. I passed by the red tent, where country music was playing, and people sang along, breaking into claps and whistles every few minutes.

I turned around and walked toward the tent, driven by a sudden desire to make my presence known. I lifted the red flap and stepped inside, where a couple was swaying drunkenly, belting out something resembling "Yesterday" by The Beatles. Middle-aged couples were pressed together. Wine glasses dangled perilously from their fingers. Children ran through the tent and jumped around holding hands, all joy and motion and eagerness. I realized after a moment that I had stepped into a wedding reception. I leaned against a wall. In the midst of family, I was anonymous. I left unnoticed.

A single seagull sat on the beach, facing the ocean. The smoke of the sunset had cleared. Soon there would be nothing left to see.

I found Simon on an isolated patch a mile from the hotel. His fishing rod hung limply from his hand. He was smoking a cigarette, inhaling with deep reverence the tiny torch with a faint flame at its end. His veneration for it made me want to hold one myself, as though we were in vigil. The light disappeared into the chunk of ash.

"Fish aren't biting," he said.

"Maybe they've gotten savvy," I said.

"How was it?" He stepped toward me.

I shook my head.

He reached over to squeeze my hand. "Leela, I wish I knew what questions to ask you."

"No one knows what to say after someone dies."

"I'm not talking about just now. I mean always. I wish I knew how to know you. To speak your language."

"Me too," I whispered. I rested my cheek, briefly, against the broadness of his back. And, for a second, he was no longer the illusory Simon Le Bon. He put out the cigarette and got down on his hands and knees, collecting brown and white pebbles from the sand. He flung a pebble into the sea, then another. I expected them to skip gracefully against the water's surface, but each brushed the surface and then sank.

"Maybe it's not about asking the *right* questions," I said finally. A massive, unwieldy rock sat at my feet. I bent over and picked it up with some effort.

"What do you mean?" He asked.

I flung it into the water, underhanded. The water splashed, slapping us in the face as the rock landed with a disgruntled thump. We began to laugh. Then Simon collected his gear, and we walked back to the hotel, hand in hand. He held his fishing rod in his other hand, like a cane in the sand.

"I mean," I said, "that maybe the problem is that we've stopped asking questions at all. Because we're afraid to admit what we don't know."

We hadn't walked together, side by side, for so long that we collided often. "How did our bodies fit so well together during sex," I said, laughing, "when we can't stop bumping into each other?" And before he said anything I realized it—our bodies hadn't aligned properly during lovemaking since we'd started to know, actually know, one another.

"Well, maybe it's okay to have bumpy sex for a while."

"Maybe. What's the name of this shell?" I asked, shining my flashlight down on the sand.

He knelt down. "I really don't know."

We kept walking. "Is that the Big Dipper?" I asked, pointing into the distance.

"Leela, I have no fucking clue," he said, doing his best Simon Le Bon accent.

I smiled. "You know you're actually nothing like Simon Le Bon," I said.

"Oh, I know it. And you are definitely no Natalie Portman."

We couldn't stop laughing. I could keep making Simon up, filling in the gaps through the prescriptions I'd filled for him. That was what my parents had done after all—lapsed into silence. Stopped asking the uncomfortable questions. Or we could revel in all that was unknown, mysterious to both of us. And find a way to create our own language.

When we arrived back at our hotel room Simon fell asleep, his arm slung over my chest. His body was warm, substantial. Real. So many nights I had stayed up, trying to match my breathing to his. But I could never quite keep pace with his quick inhalations. That night, for the first time in many months, I let myself breathe naturally. And I slept deeply, and well.

My mother fetched us before dawn, and we dragged ourselves downstairs to a van labeled "Dolphin Expedition." As we crawled into the back seat, the other passengers, a couple and their child, sang their hellos.

"You here on vacation?" The man asked. He wore a Hawaiian shirt unbuttoned to midway down his chest. His wife wore a tight pink halter top and obscenely bright orange lipstick. The boy swayed back and forth with impatience.

"No," my mother spoke up. "My husband died. We were very much in love—"

"That sucks," the wife said, cutting her off. My mother sat back, visibly annoyed, and I covered a smile with my hand. I wrapped my arm around her shoulder.

The woman went on: "Last night, we were just trying to play our guitar by the hotel pool, and these people *complained.* Such *prudes.*"

"Yeah," her son repeated. "Total *prudes.*"

When we arrived, we were guided to a boat, and we sat on the sides as it whirred through the water. The breeze was cool on our faces, and when I looked at Simon he was smiling. We both were. The Prudes' son refused to take off his cowboy hat, and he waved his arms over the side of the boat, chanting "DolphinsDolphinsDolphinsDolphinsDolphins" until the hat was swept into the water, and he broke into tears. After a while the boat paused in the water, and the instructors helped us put on our goggles and gear.

"Will the dolphins come to us?" My mom asked, worry straining her face.

"Dolphins are very warm and friendly," the instructor said. "They love people. They get excited whenever they see humans, and they show it by spinning."

The instructor dropped a microphone into the water, and a deep, elephant-like moan vibrated through the water. "That's the song of a humpback whale," she said. "Every mating season, a new male creates a unique song, and the rest of the whales echo it. You can hear it from miles away. It always sounds closer than it actually is."

"It sounds like Chewbacca from *Star Wars*," The Prudes' son said.

"Time to get in the water," the instructor said.

We dangled our legs over the side of the boat as the instructors nudged us into the water, one by one. As the instructor prodded the Prudes into the ocean, I felt sick, as though we were all being forced into a mass grave. The bodies toppled over and splashed in the water.

"We'll meet back here," Simon whispered, standing behind me. Then it was my turn, and after the initial shock the water was surprisingly warm. The snorkeling mask was tight on my face, and I tugged on it. "Heads down," the instructor shouted from the boat. "You'll miss the dolphins if you keep looking up. Stay underwater."

Legs flailed underwater, indistinct as strands of seaweed. My mom was behind me, pulling at my ankles. She said: "You can't leave me alone."

"You need to look for them yourself," I said, squeezing her arm. "You'll survive without me."

I pulled the mask over my face and dipped my head underwater, moving my legs like scissors to propel myself forward. My breath emerged in short gasps. When I came up from underneath the surface, Simon bobbed in the distance. Or at least I thought it was him. I couldn't pick him out definitively from the rest of the bodies encased in life vests. I waved in his general direction, then swam on.

The song of a whale vibrated through the water, a deep, definitive sound, and I felt a sudden chill. I ducked my head back under the surface with my eyes wide open, while the mournful wail shook the waters. I wanted, more than anything, to be engulfed in the haunting music.

The whale could have been miles away, I knew, but I thrashed toward the source of that howl. The ocean trembled, and then, just as suddenly, the rumble was gone. The others were even farther away, and I realized I'd been swimming in the other direction from them for some time.

I ducked below the surface again, and below me a school of six dolphins swam like a mirage before the ocean swallowed them up. I followed them, my arms making wide arcs. But they'd soon disappeared. In the distance, I heard the Prudes yelp with delight as the dolphins sprang up around them, spinning up in the air.

Around me the ocean was vast and thick and unknowable. I wondered if the dolphins gravitated toward all humans, or whether they approached only those who were fully alive. I imagined my father bobbing in the water with a lifejacket, waiting for the dolphins to come. Perhaps they'd sense he had left most of himself behind in that childhood home in Kolkata filled with handmade kites, and they'd swim past him, dismissing him as a corpse.

The others climbed back into the boat, ending their courtship of the dolphins. My mother and Simon waved, gesturing at me to swim back. I waved in return. I would rejoin them soon. But for now I paddled further away and waited, hoping that the whale would continue singing its raw, haunting song, and the dolphins would spin above the water in a magnificent display of camaraderie, pronouncing in their emphatic dance: *You are not yet dead.*

Tita Norma Wore a Headscarf

Katherinna Mar

Two hunched-over, broken-down, little old brown ladies amble up your block. Their wrinkled heads wrapped in wool scarves, their tiny bodies tucked tight beneath thrift store coat upon thrift store coat—they're bible thumpers, the most forlorn kind. They're Been-There Done-That Born-Again evangelists, Women of The Lord who were once women of the flesh.

Gusts of winter wind blow their coats open and the scarves off their heads and you worry that their small frail bodies will be swept away. But they are sticky like spilt Sunday mass wine, they have stuck to this neighborhood every Sunday for decades, and they are here to redeem souls like coupons.

The man down the block, with his blonde burly beard and a COEXIST bumper sticker on his Subaru, he slams his front door hard in their faces. As does the new age Buddhist girl with a lotus-flower tattoo behind her ear, who has just returned from a trip to Tibet. The other night, she'd come over with a bottle of wine to explain her newfound understanding of the nature of Tibetan oppression, how her new-found enlightenment helped her transcend jet lag. And the mother of the blue-eyed twins across the way? She says loud and proud, "get off my property, morons."

In fact, every one of your neighbors slams their door in their faces. Realizing they are losing this crusade, these missionaries take out their cell phones and dial frantically.

Reinforcements arrive.

Soon the whole neighborhood is rife with saintly saved women, their tote bags overflowing with holy books and xeroxed pamphlets. Bibles are tossed back and forth over awnings like hot potatoes, curses are shouted from inside doorways, and all these old women do is wave goodbye. Yell, "have a blessed day."

When those two little old ladies finally hobble up to your apartment, you hide. Turn out all your lights. Close all your curtains. Collapse into a ball and shiver in the corner as the doorbell strikes again and again like the last call for Sunday service. Each ding makes your heart shake and you bunch up tighter hoping they won't, like a god-given miracle, find their way in.

You knew converts like them before. Women who'd held their tongues tight their entire lives, like your childhood friend's once-sensible mother from Kingstown who could not hold down a man, like your beloved high school biology teacher from Jakarta who'd learned English reading Darwin, like your second cousin from Cebu who came here for a future and now speaks of nothing but the Second Coming. Once, these were women you loved to talk with, but soon enough they were women who neither laughed nor cried but told only stories of how they were saved. You wonder what changed them, who changed them.

After fifteen minutes, the two women retreat. At the first knock, you'd quietly crept up to your peephole to find them holding hands in prayer, pounding on the door with the heavy crucifixes that weighed down their necks. You only saw the tops of their covered heads and the wrinkled skin of their mangled hands. When you no longer heard their knocking or footsteps you opened the door quietly to make sure they were really gone and find they've tacked a pamphlet to it. A written reminder that you can hide from them only for as long as you can hide from God.

You shake it off. Later that night you go to the block potluck and everyone is tittering about this Sunday's spectacle. The mother of the twins asks the room, who do they think they are, anyway? They must be kept away from sensible children. The lotus flower neighbor laughs that next time she sees them, she'll invite them in for a meditation on the power of the goddess and the sanctity of quiet Sunday afternoons. You take the blonde bearded man home because on some nights you coexist in the same bed, and as you watch him sleep he comes to look like a stranger you once wanted to punch in the face.

The next morning the pamphlet is still on your kitchen counter and you smirk, shove it into a drawer already too heavy with fast food delivery menus. You think about the movie *Deliverance*, the eeriness of it, then you think about the word itself, and then the women with their bibles fade out of your memory.

Soon enough, though, through the grapevine you'll hear that one of those women was Tita Norma. The other? Your mother. When they knock again next Sunday, you'll find yourself hiding again. Peeking from behind the window curtain, you'll watch your mother shrink as she walks away in defeat. You'll hide and think a good daughter would open that door, but a better mother would not have run off in the middle of the night with a new God.

You think it would be best to place yourself in front of her pounding little fists that thump *salvation*, that tap tap tap *submit to Jesus*, yet you hide in the tiny tile corner like you're hiding from the devil, a midday glass of wine in hand, not the blood of Christ nor the Eucharist.

Months later, after hundreds of knocks, maybe thousands, after you can no longer order Tom Yum soup or Dim Sum or even a deep dish pizza because the guilt of shutting your mother's happiness into a menu drawer finally starts to get to you, you'll finally open the door for her. Drown her in excuses. How would I have known it was you? And wasn't it you who taught me to never answer the door for strangers?

How did you even know I was home? And what are you doing out in this Chicago cold again, anyway? Seeking salvation for Tita Norma? Don't you know you'll never find it?

She'll say she is out here in this cold praying for you. That when she prayed for you before, to the old god, the deaf one, it was clear he hadn't heard—she'd prayed to him every day for decades and still, your Tita Norma remains unwell. Your brother is still unmarried. And you, my dear daughter, are just a tramp.

She'll leave you with another pamphlet, you'll worry about her health but worry more at your own silly fear. Since when does *Christ* frighten you, you'll ask yourself. And since when do you hide from little old ladies?

Mom had secrets like you wouldn't believe. She came to the States with one little suitcase, now shoved into the back of a closet, held quiet with a tiny lock. When I was kid I once tried to pry it open, but she stormed into the bedroom, smacked me across the face and said, "you'll never get it open, I've swallowed the key." I leafed through my parents' dusty old photo albums trying to find her face couched between those of her family's, round sepia faces, I imagined, ones I'd never seen. I left all those photos back home, she said. And the typhoon swept them to sea.

After twenty years I still couldn't name all of her siblings, when I asked what neighborhood she grew up in she only said the outskirts of Manila, and every long distance collect call she accepted brought her voice down to a toothy whisper.

The only things I do know about Mom are the things I have seen—for decades she prayed to her childhood god for her daughter, her son, and Tita Norma. Most days, she laid out dinners for dead relatives and when they were finished eating, she tossed the leftovers out the door to feed the neighborhood strays. Every day, she attended six a.m. mass and was home in time to cook breakfast. Before meals, she made the sign of the cross so often and fast that sometimes I grew dizzy. The only possessions that seemed to mean much to her were an assortment of Virgin Mary statuettes, a stack of prayer cards, a holy bible, and a trunk-sized collection of rosaries.

Our house was Mom's own little church. Throughout the years, she'd become the neighborhood women's nondenominational sage, the house a place for them to scream salvation, or simply to scream. When our young Korean next-door neighbor needed advice on how to quiet her surly old husband, she came to Mom's table. When Natalya, the mother of seven from down the block, found herself finally with an empty home, it was Mom's couch she came to sit on and wet with fat tears. When Ellen from Ireland's fourteen-year-old daughter got knocked up, she and Mom prayed rosaries for days. All the neighborhood women had come to our door at least once, and Mom took on the celestial glow of the Holy Mother.

Mom may have been holy but she wasn't a preacher. She was quiet with downcast eyes, she was well-behaved and took instruction. She got by by not getting in the way. For example, at the mall one day a man with a burly blonde beard walked up to us and asked where in the world my father was, thinking maybe he'd get laid. Mom smiled, ignoring his plain audacity and said I'm sure you're a nice man, but I am not interested. He followed behind us as far as the lingerie store. Then in the food court, a mother with skin the color and pallor of the soft serve ice cream I was eating, sat down beside us and scolded, don't you know it's wrong to give a child dessert for lunch? Mom took the cone out of my hand and thanked her, waited to give it back until the woman walked away. By the time we were at the cash register at Kohl's, about to pay for my new school clothes, I was praying. I prayed as the pimply employee cut up our credit card, as she muttered "stupid chink," as my mother apologized profusely, making the sign of the cross, I prayed that we could become shrouded and unseen. Mom took my hand and the hangers of clothes and put everything back where it came from, smoothed creases, flipped over price tags, saying not a word but squeezing my knuckles white.

She never did get to tell that man that dad was at home in front of the TV, or the scolding mother that ice cream is a perfectly suitable meal for a child, especially on a Saturday, or the pimply cashier that a cut up credit card was better than no card at all.

You visit another country and you have to respect its customs, Mom always said. Here in the States, she respected customs so obediently that she'd become them. She wasn't even a visitor anymore, she had the papers and the wedding ring and the two half-white children to prove it. The only things from the old world Mom openly displayed were her Catholicism (vehemently), her accent (unwillingly), and her desire for a material comfort that did not contradict her work ethic or piety.

So on the day I met Tita Norma, I was not surprised that this oldest friend I'd never met lived just down the street. My secretive mother was full of surprises.

Back then, Tita Norma lived with her daughter in the subsidized housing behind Comeback Covenant, though the two didn't pray to that god or anyone like him. Tita Norma and her daughter worshipped facing east, bowing and saying prayers under their breaths, five times a day.

Mom had warned me that if they got up for prayer during our visit, I was to wait politely and look away. Mom had also warned me not to play dress-up with Tita Norma's daughter. No dresses no scarves no makeup no nothing. They are going against God and I don't want nothing to do with it, she'd said.

The apartment was seven stories up a crumbling staircase and as

Mom and I climbed, I could feel her start to shake. Even now, I still forget it's not heights she's afraid of. At the top of the stairs, we didn't have to knock. Norma stood outside her door and seemed to quiver with impatience. She grabbed Mom and squeezed her until her shaking ceased.

Tita Norma wore a headscarf. She tied it under her chin as she beckoned us inside. She pulled it over the bruise on her cheekbone, tugged it over the purple thumbprint on her chubby neck, tucked her stray hairs under its shroud. Smiling serenely at my mother, who she hadn't seen in years, she began to babble on in a muted frenzy until Mom stopped her mile a minute mouth. No hablo espanol, Norma. Y, you know that.

Ya allah Norma said under her breath. I forgot. Your mom and I are like sisters, from other mothers. From other countries! she said to me. Norma was ecstatic. Boisterous. So excited I thought she'd burst through her own skin. Before we slid off our shoes to come in, Mom asked her, are you sure he won't be here?

Beneath her head covering, Tita Norma's long, thick braid rebelled. She raised me into her lap to appraise this best friend's child she was only now meeting, and I thought I could use that braid to lower myself out the window. From then on, for the rest of my life, Rapunzel was short and stout and Salvadorena with a jet-black mane.

Aziza! Ven aqui! Tita Norma yelled. A frail girl came out of her bedroom, wearing a headscarf, too. Hers was white, without wrinkles, its edges embroidered with pearls. It tightly circled her perfect face. Norma's daughter was impossibly pale, her thick kohl eyeliner and dangling gold earrings betrayed that she was only ten years old. A preteen angel nymph. A Muslim Virgin Mary. You two will be friends like Ladylyn and I are friends, Tita Norma said and gave us both the once over. Aziza said to me, Nice to meet you. I'm moving soon. As if to say, no. We won't be.

Mom and Norma sat down at the kitchen table and shooed us away. Before Aziza relented, she grabbed two yellow onions from the pantry, peeled their skins off with her fingers and held one out to me, taking a bite into the other. No thanks, I looked at her skeptically. Suit yourself, she said. But it's just like an apple, only sweeter.

In the living room, Aziza sat down on the opposite end of the plastic-covered couch. She couldn't stop talking about her new family, the new house they were moving into, the shiny new neighborhood in the city's northern suburbs.

The house has a swimming pool. And a basketball court for Mohammed.

Who's Mohammed?

Aziza rolled her eyes and said, my brother.

What color is the house?

White.

How big is it?

Bigger than this place. Bigger than your place.

You've never been to my place.

Somehow, I just know that it's bigger.

How many rooms?

I don't know, fifteen?

Can I visit you when you move in? She had to think about this for a while.

No, she said, and adjusted her earrings, tugged at her headscarf.

Tita Norma's living room was stacked high with cardboard boxes. The boxes stood collecting dust, daily reminding Norma of everything she was about to lose. Those layers of dust served as reminders that all she had cherished could be packed away for ages, neglected and useless. Porcelain trinkets dusted daily, hand-polished silver serving ware, Aziza's toys sprayed in disinfectant, her husband's trousers that she herself had pressed, all her fine wifely work was now being moved to a big house, far away, without her.

In the kitchen, Norma was doubled over the table, sobbing into her fists, and Mom was doubled over Norma, hugging her and petting what was exposed of her hair. The knot of Norma's headscarf loosened under Mom's touch.

Don't mind her. She's always crying these days, Aziza said of her mother as she lined my eyelids black.

She doesn't want to leave?

That's not it. She's not coming anyway. Come now. I want to show them your new look.

Long before Aziza and I were born, Tita Norma and Mom lived together. They were inseparable friends. Both colonized by the Spaniards (who by the way, they adored), both devout Catholics, both with mouths full of shit-talk about their respective homelands; both their mouths were parched and unsated until they came to the States, they said.

They had also had their differences. Norma was boy crazy and Mom was ambitious. Mom wanted a life all her own and Norma wanted to share: her food, her clothes, her affection. Mom imagined her life in the States would go by busy and professional and in an instant, like a three minute long pop song or a commercial for a chemical disinfectant. Norma pictured, however irrationally, a life of American immortality. Mom went to bed praying, Norma fell asleep dreaming.

Back in the day, Mom and Norma were hot. Sriracha and Cholula, their young admirers thought. Ginger and cayenne. Norma's face was perfectly round and brown and the whites of her eyes left you feeling unholy. Mom's lips were full and thick but red like Mary Magdalene's sin. But, always the delicacy and never the dish. A man could stuff his mouth full of potatoes and pretzels and Pillsbury, after all, but their mothers had warned against swallowing fiery peppers by the fistful.

Would they be able to handle the burn?

Mom and Tita Norma's favorite bar was the Night Cap. They'd pinky sworn to only date American men, who were better-educated and purportedly more polite than the apes back home. The Night Cap was a typical Chicago dive, the sort you used to see on every other unassuming street corner, but it was full of young doctors and lawyers and engineers who worked long hard days and went to bed alone. Every Saturday night when the seedy place was cleared of tables to reveal a dance floor, stuck with gum and cigarette butts and just a hint of last weekend's trash, Norma and Mom were always first up to dance. Singing Abba in their silly accents. Giggling like country school girls because that's what they'd been before they were green card-wielding immigrants. Dancing in their awkward, sex-censored Catholic way, short stout bodies emulating tall lanky blondes. All eyes were on them.

Then came the men, their stiff narrow hips shimmying embarrassment, circling the two in an awkward courtship ritual, offering love or affection or devotion or money. Mom and Tita Norma would go out for a drink and come home full of six, not a dime of their own money spent. Mom only revelled in the money she'd saved. Norma went home and carefully considered each drunken proposal.

When Sunday morning rolled around, Mom would be dressed for church, shaking Norma awake, reminding her that the men she'd fawned over last night were no replacement for the one who created them.

When Norma's steady American boyfriend left her for a pale dumpling of a woman, Norma was devastated. I'll marry anything that walks! she declared. He turned out to be the owner of the Night Cap.

It was a good match. Mr. El Adawy was handsome and Tita Norma was loyal. Mr. El Adawy was frugal, had put away a considerable amount of money to start a family, and Norma was tired of working. The only condition of their marriage was that Tita Norma convert.

There were lots of things about Norma that Mom could tolerate, but this was not one.

What about that Pole from the pub? I see him eyeing you, his eyes are blue. SO blue. He's an engineer. And a Catholic. Mom pleaded.

No Ladylyn. I've made up my mind.

So, you like men from the Mid East? How about that Lebanese? He's a doctor, Norma. A doctor. Who cares about his hook nose? A doctor and a Christian.

Ladylyn. Give it up.

So Mom did. Mom and Norma packed up Norma's belongings and after one last hand holding prayer Norma moved out of Mom's apartment and in with Mr. El Adawy. Mom attended the wedding, silently praying for Norma's soul the entire time, and didn't see her again until Norma was in her forties and wearing a headscarf.

In the kitchen, Mom and Tita Norma ignored our pleas for attention. Perhaps they hadn't heard us, so locked were their eyes on one another. Aziza took me into her bedroom, crowded with boxes like a corn maze.

Mom talks about your mom all the time, Aziza said.

What does she say? I wondered.

That she abandoned her the same way Dad did.

It wasn't just Norma's converted soul that Mom worried over every day for a decade. My mother had suspected all along that Mr. El Adawy would one day save up enough to afford a second wife. At the kitchen table, Mom's bright eyes brimmed with I-Told-You-So's as she listened to Tita Norma.

Mr. El Adawy was not a hitter but Tita Norma had driven him to do what any man would have done, Tita Norma said. The bruise on her cheek and the thumbprint on her neck were her own fault. She'd known all along that the day would come. If only she'd prepared, if only she'd had time to prepare. Always so busy with her two young children and her endless store of in-laws, the past ten years had gone past in an instant. Most of her time was spent appeasing her youngest sister in-law who found her cooking atrocious, her oldest brother in-law who believed his niece and nephew would grow up godless, and her ancient mother-in-law who expressed disappointment in harsh muttered consonants that Tita Norma did not understand. Norma's own children always sided with their father and their father, once valiant and straight-spined, turned out to be both the family pushover and it's articulator of Norma's flaws. She went through her married days a lone whirlwind, and her only times of peace were her three-minute intervals of prayer.

Norma's husband had not mentioned the other woman. He'd simply said, we're moving. It's time. Norma wailed for days, looking to her children for comfort. Perhaps they were too young to understand their mother's sorrow, or too excited to leave their cramped apartment, but they would be the first to tell you that their mother was a nut. And any onlooker would believe the children, as she now spent her days pressing pants and packing boxes like a swift, obsessive robot.

In Norma's kitchen that day, Mom was ecstatic that she would finally have her Norma back. She sat on her hands that held a peace offering: a rosary with the tiniest crucifix. But When Norma announced she was leaving Mr. El Adawy and not Allah, Mom was confused. She said a quick Hail Mary then, but wasn't it this God who caused all your sorrows? Wasn't the God we shared before your marriage much more kind? Forgiving? Generous?

No. Norma said. You are wrong. Your god gave me nothing but grief. This one now gives me peace.

Now that she was proceeding with a divorce, giving up her son and daughter and nagging in-laws, her husband and her housework and her weekly allowance, Norma found solace in prayer.

Meanwhile, Aziza unpacked boxes and draped scarves over me.

First, I was a mummy. Then, I was a misshapen tent. Finally, I was her sister, she said, my hair covered, my earlobes pierced through with a safety pin, swollen but bejewelled by two little pearls.

When Aziza and I finally emerged from the bedroom, Mom's face was sour and her shoes were already on. Say goodbye to Aziza, she said.

Mom dragged me home in silence, in shock at having Tita Norma for only a moment after so long, at my head in a hijab. "Listen, anak," she said, turning to Tagalog the way she always did when serious. "One day, you'll fall in love with a man. This man will try to erase your past and make your life his own. He will convince you he loves you and you'll believe him. But one day, without notice, for no reason, he will hate you and throw you away. You'll have to start over again and you might not be able to. By then, you might be too old. Too rundown. Do you understand?" She asked.

You mean like you and dad?

No, that's not what I mean. She sighed. That is different. Your father is a good man. No passion, no lies. A Catholic. She said.

So you mean like Tita Norma and Mr. El Adawy?

Exactly. Her shoulders dropped in relief.

Aziza says Tita Norma is just an idiot. She doesn't have to give up her family. She wants to.

Mom turned to me, her face contorted. Her hand stiffened and stung my cheek, making the same noise it did when she anxiously slapped her palms together in prayer. I tugged Aziza's scarf off, letting it trail behind me before I dropped it into the street.

Mom didn't mention Tita Norma again for almost twenty years. After that visit, we returned to life as usual. I do suspect that the person who dialed our number daily, only to hang up when someone answered, was Norma, her voice stuck indefinitely in her throat. I often wondered about her, about how often, if at all, she saw her daughter. If she stayed on in that dismal apartment alone. If she'd remarried, if she'd shed her headscarf.

It wasn't long after Mom was priced out of the neighborhood that I moved back into it. Mom's old home, her own little church, was gutted and aired out, its only parishioners a family that does not pray to any god. Sometimes, during these Sunday spectacles, I think about knocking on my old door.

By the time Tita Norma attended her first service at the Comeback Covenant, Mom's faith was already on the outs. Dad was gone, her children had left and neglected her, she could no longer afford the home she'd made. Like a broken wind-up doll, she started attending mass several times a day, writing notes on post-it's of sins she may have forgotten to confess, until her bedroom wall was covered in blaring neon squares, her prayers unanswered, her body unable to leave bed. When her lease ended she tore the notes off the wall one by one and burned them.

Then one day Tita Norma came knocking, more than fifteen years late. Mom thought she was seeing a ghost. My best friend I've looked for you everywhere! she squealed. And by then Mom was ready for a new life.

It started with a Saturday luncheon, packed with old ladies from all corners of the earth. Then came the sermon, delivered by a man with a voice like an angel, a body like a Greek myth, a smile that had these old ladies melting in their chairs. He espoused universal love and tolerance and the power of the Woman, the duty of the Woman to spread God's word. He hearkened to their suffering, their pain, their loss. He listened, nodded understanding, which was the most any man had ever offered any one of them. He armed them with pamphlets and tiny bibles and let loose his missionary army.

Tita Norma went out into the cold a new woman but continued to wear her headscarf. At first, Mom didn't get it. Wrapped up in these scarves was a history of pretty women concealing their wild manes. But by then she knew better than to say anything.

One Sunday morning, I invited the two old ladies in for tea. Tita Norma greeted me like no time had passed, like I was family. I came to know that Tita Norma never visited our churchly home because she simply was not allowed there. Not by her husband, who worried Mom would turn her back, and not by my mother, who held a grudge bigger than her faith, big enough that she'd replaced her oldest friend with a pious memory. My mother had made it her mission to remove that gauzy mess from Tita Norma's head. She was willing to take her time if she had to. She would ultimately lose.

I wanted to hear Tita Norma talk about those lost decades between her and my mother. I wanted to hear her ask my mom, "did La Virgen not wear a mantle? Do nuns not hide their heads in fear of god and men? Do you not hide as well, when you put curlers in your hair? And this whole story you pity me for? Of my family leaving without so much as a thank you? What had that to do with my headscarf? Family abandons, god abandons. Your tongue is kept tied, your thoughts kept to yourself, you're either wearing a headscarf or not."

But Tita Norma didn't need to ask. Mom finally understood. It only took a lifetime. It was why now she evangelized at my door, at my neighbors' doors, why now she spewed every aching word held tight in her chest for decades out to the world, into anyone who would listen. It was why now she walked with Tita Norma instead of with the memory of her. The Comeback evangelists were not spreading the word of God. They were spreading the stories of themselves.

Tita Norma wore a headscarf. She tied it under her chin. It detracted from the crow's feet that grew out the corners of her eyes. It hid her thick silvery braid. She spoke soft and fast but proud behind her headscarf as she told stories to unkind strangers. At times, it fell over her wide open eyes, whose whites, now yellow, vowed you were unholy but still young.

Contributors

Yvette Benavides hails from the border city of Laredo, Texas. She is a professor of English at Our Lady of the Lake University in San Antonio, a book critic for the *San Antonio Express News* and commentator on Texas Public Radio. She is also a regular contributing columnist for *The Rivard Report*. She is the 2015 recipient of the Artist Foundation of San Antonio literary arts award. Her short fiction has been published in *The Linden Avenue, SOL: English Writing Mexico, Bellevue Literary Review* and *Huizache*.

Amy Elizabeth Bishop is a recent graduate of the State University of New York, Geneseo. She currently works as an assistant at Dystel & Goderich Literary Management in NYC and reads for *Wyvern Lit* and *The Rumpus*. Her poetry has or will appear in *Gandy Dancer, The Susquehanna Review*, and *Dialogist*. On Twitter at @givealittlelove.

Christopher Carmona first collection of short stories entitled, *The Road to Llorona Park* was published by Stephen F. Austin University Press in 2016. He has recently edited an anthology called *Outrage: A Protest Anthology about Injustice in a Post 9/11 World* and was a co-editor for *The Beatest State In The Union: An Anthology of Beat Texas Writing*. He has two collections of poetry: *beat* and *I Have Always Been Here*. Finally, he is the Artistic Director of the Coalition of New Chican@ Artists.

Fiona Cheong is the author of the *Scent Of The Gods* (w.w. norton, 1991) and *Shadow Theatre* (soho, 2002). Her shorter work can be found in *Charlie Chan Is Dead: An Anthology of Contemporary Asian American Literature* and *Tilting The Continent: Southeast Asian American Writing.* A native of Singapore, she presently teaches in the graduate writing program at the University of Pittsburgh.

Alexandria Delcourt finished her MFA at Stonecoast in 2014 and is currently an Inclusive Excellence Fellow at the University of Wisconsin-Whitewater. Her work has been used in dance performances, read internationally, and has appeared in *Written River*, *Poetry Quarterly*, *As/Us: A Space for Women of the World*, *Kalyani Magazine*, *FULCRUM: An Annual of Poetry and Aesthetics*, and other publications. She lives in Madison, Wisconsin.

Araceli Esparza writes bilingual-bicultural picture books in between parenting, teaching and saving words for later. She holds an MFA from Hamline University and was named 2015 Women to Watch For by Brava Magazine. FollowBack @WI_MUJER for diverse literature news and bookish things.

Andrée Greene is a graduate of Cornell (BA) and Columbia (MFA, fiction) Universities. She lives in New York City where she teaches creative writing, is a freelance editor, and recently completed her novel, *Nobody's Doll.*

Cathy Guo is a student and writer working on her first chapbook project funded by Columbia University, which aims to present oral history and poetry together in a dialogue on memory, landscape and diaspora in modern Chinese history. @_duxfemina_

Leticia Hernández-Linares is a poet, interdisciplinary artist, and educator. She has performed her poemsongs throughout the country and in El Salvador. The author of *Mucha Muchacha, Too Much Girl* (Tía Chucha Press, 2015), her writing appears in newspapers, literary journals, and anthologies, some of which include: *U.S. Latino Literature Today, Street Art San Francisco, Pilgrimage, Huizache,* and *This Bridge We Call Home*. She lives, works, and writes in the Mission District, San Francisco—20 years strong. Visit her at: joinleticia.com

H. N. Holder was born in Trinidad and Tobago and has been writing fiction and poetry since 2007. She's published three short stories: "The Iridescent Blue-Black Boy with Wings," "Love Story No. 8: Jane and Phillip," and "Keepsake." When not writing fiction and poetry about love and the grotesque, Holder blogs about teaching and learning.

Didi Jackson's poems have appeared in *Ploughshares, Passages North, Green Mountain Review,* and *The Café Review*, among other publications. Her recent chapbook, *Slag & Fortune*, was published by Floating Wolf Quarterly. She divides her time between Vermont and Florida, teaching humanities at the University of Central Florida and poetry and the visual arts at the University of Vermont.

Ani Kazarian writes essays, short stories, and screenplays, and is at work on her first novel. Her research interests include literature, culture, history, and trauma. She lives in Los Angeles with her husband.

Erin Koehler, born and raised outside Rochester, New York, graduated from SUNY Geneseo in 2015. Her poetry has appeared in *Terrain, The Susquehanna Review, Gandy Dancer*, and as a selection in the *Adroit Journal* Editor's List for the 2015 Prize for Poetry. Koehler resides in Boston where she hopes to pursue a career writing children's literature.

Dr. Raina J. León is a Cave Canem graduate fellow, CantoMundo fellow, and member of the Carolina African American Writers Collective. Her collections of poetry include *Canticle of Idols*, *Boogeyman Dawn*, and *sombra :(dis)locate*. She is a founding editor of *The Acentos Review*, an online quarterly devoted to the promotion and publication of LatinX arts. She is an Associate Professor of education at Saint Mary's College of California.

Katherinna Mar is a writer based in Chicago. She's currently an MFA candidate at Bennington College.

Keya Mitra is currently an assistant professor of creative writing and literature at Pacific University and graduated in 2010 with a doctorate from the University of Houston's Creative Writing Program, where she also earned her MFA. In 2008, Keya spent a year in India on a Fulbright grant in creative writing. Keya's fiction has appeared in *The Kenyon Review*, *Arts and Letters*, *The Bellevue Literary Review*, *The Southwest Review*, *Slush Pile*, *Best New American Voices*, *Ontario Review*, *The Journal of Commonwealth and Postcolonial Studies*, *Orchid*, *Event*, *Fourteen Hills*, *Torpedo*, and *Confrontation*. She has completed a novel as well as a short-story collection and memoir.

Robin Scofield, author of *And the Ass Saw the Angel* and *Sunflower Cantos* (Mouthfeel Press), has poems appearing in *The Malpais Review*, *The Texas Weather Anthology*, and *Pilgrimage*. Her next full-length collection, *Drive*, comes out in 2016. She is poetry editor for *BorderSenses* and writes with the Tumblewords Project in El Paso, where she lives with her husband and her Belgian Shepherd.

Grace Singh Smith was born and raised in Assam, India; she currently lives in Santa Monica and works at Santa Monica College as its spokesperson. Her short stories have appeared in the *Santa Monica Review* and *Cleaver Magazine*. Smith is an MFA (fiction) candidate at Bennington College, and is at work on her first novel.

Kelsey Valadez's writing can be found at adaphora.wordpress.com

Editors

Angie Cruz is an Assistant Professor of English at the University of Pittsburgh and is the author of two novels, *Soledad*, and *Let It Rain Coffee*. She was recently awarded the Elizabeth K. Doenges Visiting Artist/Scholar Fellowship from Mary Baldwin College and is at work on her third novel.

Oindrila Mukherjee has an MFA from the University of Florida and a Ph.D. in Creative Writing from the University of Houston. Oindrila worked as a journalist in Calcutta. Her fiction was most recently published in *Indian Voices*, an anthology of emerging Indian writers from around the world. She is an Assistant Professor at Grand Valley State University.

Special thanks to our contributing editors in poetry:

Suzannah Spaar was born and raised in Charlottesville, Virginia. She received her BA in English from the University of Chicago and is an MFA Candidate in Poetry at the University of Pittsburgh.

Lucia C LoTempio hails from Buffalo, NY and is currently an instructor and MFA candidate in Poetry at the University of Pittsburgh. She is a sucker for tiny animals and tiny babies. She was a finalist for the *Black Warrior Review* 10th Annual Contest in Poetry and for the

Winter Tangerine Annual Awards. Lucia counts for VIDA and is on the advisory board for *Gandy Dancer*.

Acknowledgments

"Love Story for a Foreign Girl" by Feona Cheong, originally pubilshed in *East Lit* © 2015 by Feona Cheong. Reprinted by permission of author.

"Strange Leaves" by Christopher Carmona, originally published in The *Texas Observer* © 2014 by Christopher Carmon.
Reprinted by permission of the author.

"Almost Animal" by Didi Jackson, originally published in
The Common © 2015 by Didi Jackson.
Reprinted by permission of author.

Thanks to:

Layout/design extraordinaire (and then some), Adriana E. Ramírez; Managing Editor, Joshua Graber (and the University of Pittsburgh English Department); As well as all our Contributing and Advisory Editors—especially, Norma Cantú and Emily Raboteau.

www.ingramcontent.com/pod-product-compliance
Lightning Source LLC
Chambersburg PA
CBHW061449210726
48287CB00007B/2425

9781942547013